ISOLATION

The Story of Isabella Rose-Eccleby

by

Joshua Meeking

Grosvenor House
Publishing Limited

This book is published by
Grosvenor House Publishing Ltd
Link House
140 The Broadway, Tolworth, Surrey, KT6 7HT.
www.grosvenorhousepublishing.co.uk

A CIP record for this book
is available from the British Library

ISBN 978-1-83975-248-3

For Kate, Hannah, Megan, Leah, Jade, Amy,
and Mr Robinson - my GCSE Drama devising group.

Chapter One

Recurring Nightmares

1: THEN

I am home, she thought, and stopped and trembled at the thought of how her home filled with all her childhood memories looked completely different. A sixteen-year-old Isabella Rose-Eccleby overlooked the brick wall that barricaded her from what was meant to be Wardle Gardens; the only means of entry being a black gate, its paint worn away by the many years it, and the house, had stood. As the shadows of the rising sun loomed over the Castlehead streets, in unison, lights shone through the windows of Wardle Gardens to the harsh outdoors, imploring Isabella to enter the grounds and find out what truly happened on that fateful night when she was six. The distance between her footing at the gate to the matte black door – which was originally an ice white – was about twenty feet. But to the entranced teen, it felt like one step. One moment at the gate, the next, at the door, passing bushes and trees that were now twigs, oblivious of a car that had crashed into the wooden garage aside the house which was built by Isabella's grandfather, and blind of two gaping holes dug within the garden six feet deep and seven feet long. She hesitated to knock at first, but bravely did so. No answer. Another knock. Again, no answer. One last knock, but still no answer. However, this time, silence spread across the atmosphere. Nothingness arose on her, her home, the street, the town, the country, the continent, and eventually, the world. That was until... BANG. From inside the house came a bang then a scream. It was the scream of Isabella Rose-Eccleby, yet her mouth was not open. Was it even her screaming?

2

It was just a silly little nightmare. It felt so real for the six-year-old Isabella Rose-Eccleby who awakened within Wardle Gardens trembling in sweat and fear, crying, and screaming for her parents.

Her father came rushing in – her mother came in after the sound of a crash – trying to calm her down by telling her that everything was going to be okay.

"It felt so real," she sniffed, her pitch high, sitting up against the backboard of her bed.

"Nightmare do, sweetie," her father, Anthony Eccleby, replied in a soothing tone. "Sometimes I..." Isabella's mother, Sharron Rose, entered, kneeling down beside her husband beside the bed which their weeping daughter sat upon. "Rose, where were you?"

"I... I don't know," Sharron said, yawning away her daze and confusion, trying to gather where she was as Anthony's attention switched back to their girl.

"I was just about to say that I have nightmares, too."

"Really?"

"We all do, darling," agreed Sharron. "Ones about events that we don't want to happen..." Her tone gradually changed from soft to a tone that made her sound like she was in another trance. She looked it, too, staring above and around her daughter's head at the walls that seemed to close in. "Ones about death; where I see *you* lying helplessly on the sitting room floor – all cut up – with blood spewing out of *your* guts, blood drooling down *your* prone body like a beautiful red waterfall. Ones about a certain girl who also has nightmares of their loved ones hanging from the ceiling, swaying back and forth with a rope around their necks as a result of their life choices." This gave the six-year-old Isabella a reason to weep even more than she already was, Anthony comforting her – edging away from his wife. Sharron's eyes then locked onto her daughter's, finally sensing the fear building up in her sinless soul. "Wh… What was I saying?"

Anthony, using his wife's confusion to send her away, strictly told her: "You said you were going back to bed."

"Oh. Erm… okay," Sharron said with no argument, rising and exiting Isabella's bedroom, crossing the carpeted landing to her and Anthony's. She looked back, the vision of her daughter and husband blocked by the partly closed door. "You sure you're alright?" Isabella gently nodded, giving her father permission to respond with a *yes* – appearing as positively okay – but inside, she was as anxious as ever.

"Is Mother okay?"

"Honestly, I don't know. I think it might just be stress, but I promise I'll have a talk with her tomorrow. I'm sure she'll be right as rain once she wakes up."

Once she wakes up.

Anthony cringed at the thought of lying to his daughter, so that's what he didn't see it as. He saw lying to his daughter as *stretching the truth*. For Isabella's sake. Because, what if Isabella knew her mother might actually be going crazy? What if this was affecting the family? What if Isabella knew that this might as well be the end of the line for Sharron Rose? That's why he *stretched the truth*.

"Okay." She positioned herself back to lying down, placing her head on the unicorn pillow, and making herself comfortable whilst Anthony stroked her head, looking at each other in the eyes as if everything was alright. "Why did I have another nightmare, Father?" she asked tiredly, stopping him in the doorway with her words just as he was about to leave.

"They just occur," he responded, turning back and sighing. "And they happen when you least expect them." He kneeled back down at her bed, restarting to stroke through her blonde hair. "But what have I told you about nightmares?"

"They wake you up," Isabella answered, dozing off, hopefully, into a dream.

"Exactly. And when they wake you up..."

"You're out of the nightmare?"

"You're out of the nightmare, yes. So when you realise that nightmares are just harmless illusions, they won't hurt you. You'll also learn that nightmares are far from reality."

3: NOW

She awakened again. This time, a day before a decade later. But this day wasn't just any old day. This was a special day. This special day was a birthday. This special day was Sharron Rose's fortieth birthday.

Her bedroom was a good size. Big enough to fit a dozen people. Against the back wall, long ways, was the single bed with pink covers stitched with golden stars, with the back wall itself being a shade of light purple – unlike the other three walls which were cream. It also had stickers of stars and planets, Minecraft, Club Penguin, and One Direction posters. This wall stood out because not only was it purple, it was actually Isabella's Wall of Wonder. A name given by Sharron – but not used until she was nine – the Wall of Wonder and Isabella were one in the same; Isabella would stick anything her heart desired on that wall: posters, stickers, who she liked, what she liked, or her interests and hobbies.

Isabella was the wonder.

Aside the bed, jamming it between itself and the back wall, by the top of the bed was a chestnut brown stand. An angel lamp stood upon the stand proud, with its open wings being the source of light and the elegant body of the mystical creature standing perfectly upright, blowing a kiss, and precisely in line with the bottom left corner of the feather-stuffed pillow. A built-in cabinet was beneath the stand, home of her sacred diary which held many of her deepest and darkest secrets, and school utensils. Next to the lamp and stand was the ceiling-high wardrobe full of knee-length skirts, smart jackets, and shirts. She would always remain smart on any occasion; nothing that would make her seem threatening to others – more like *approachable* – and in Sharron's words, *nothing skanky*. In the opposite wall was a doorway with a newly-built door nailed in, and beside it was a chest of drawers that consisted of many old dolls that hadn't been played with in years, yet looked neat enough that they would be mistaken as brand new, along with piles of VHS home video footage of taped memories that Isabella could only recall when rewatching them. The ones that included her mother were the memories she remembered most. Just like the time they all went to the beach that day. That was a good day. In fact, *that* day was the last fond memory Isabella could actually recall having with her entire family. And in the final, and bottom drawer was the family's wide collection of DVDs that would be watched every night before bed.

Saying that Isabella was good in school was easily an understatement. Another day, another A. The straight-A student – at the time of this day – studied at Castle Grange Sixth Form, a school only for the highly determined and highly elite. She wanted to study biology, psychology, and maths, hoping to make a career out of investigating and discovering new functions of the human anatomy and the organisms within.

The dream she had before awakening on this day in March, 2019, was about her being back at Thomas Hill High, on Results Day, 23rd August, standing at the great black gates of the school she cared for so deeply.

Opening that brown envelope at the main reception before exiting Thomas Hill for the final time and seeing that she had passed all of her GCSE's with all A's made her incapable of containing her excitement. She ran home. Not *ran*. Sprinted. Sprinted home like she had just found a golden ticket; sprinted home to tell Anthony that she had cleared mathematics – her father's favourite subject – with flying colours, and sprinted home to tell her mother that her little girl had passed her exams... oh, wait.

The dream felt so real. Just like the nightmares.

Scratching her head as she walked down the grand staircase of what was now her new house, Chessington Close, Isabella's long, white nightgown followed her as she walked step by step, heading down towards the main doors, and aside the grand, brown double-doors were two archways – entrances – to either side of the house; left took her into the lounge, and right took her into the kitchen and dining area.

The sixteen-year-old first entered the kitchen. The black and white tiling on the floor, that looked like she was standing on a human-sized chess board, contrasted with the smooth granite benches on top of the lower cupboards that which went around the live-or-die board game, and were the homes of tinned food, cutlery, and cooking utensils. All of this around an oak-wood dining table in the centre, with a seat at each far end.

There used to be three seats around the dining table at Wardle Gardens.

Isabella stood in the archway of the kitchen, ready to enter, somewhat amazed by the cleanliness of it all. Her *sharronisms* must have been kicking in. Sharron was a cleaning fanatic, too. Everything had their place, and if it wasn't put back exactly where it belonged, then that person – Anthony, most of the time – got the side of Sharron that made her seem like an incarnation of the devil.

Transitioning from the kitchen to the lounge with a bowl of Kellogg's Corn Flakes cupped in her hands, she stood in the archway leading to the sitting room, again, somewhat amazed at how everything looked so clean and was in the same spot. Everything was the same; the white cushioned sofa facing the fifty-inch television on the wall, the white walls, the cream carpet, the white stand next to the sofa with a vase of blooming roses standing on it at the far end of the lounge, and even the remote control was lying still on the (always) creased cushion closest to the vase which never stood completely upright like the other two pillows. Everything was the same. Apart from one thing: her mother, Sharron Rose, was nowhere to be found.

Back at Wardle Gardens, everything was the same when Sharron was somewhere to be found.

Sharron wasn't even at the far end of the couch where she always sat at the time, 8:30, to watch the *BBC Morning News* hosted by Steven Benjamin and Carly Ray. Where Sharron sat was *her spot*. Her spot because she liked the corner. Her spot, because at a time nearly a decade ago at Wardle Gardens, she said to Isabella, who played on the mat in front, that she liked the corner because she liked how comfortable it was to sit in a corner, unable to move because of how comfortable it was, because whenever she felt like standing up from the comfortable corner, she was re-entering reality and started to feel trapped. Wardle Gardens' walls would close in on her whenever she stood, hearing the voice of her mother in her head assuring her that she had made the wrong decisions in life.

"*I like this corner, this corner* because *I feel free in my imagination*," was what Sharron had really said.

Isabella would do the same as her mother, sit in that spot, feeling evermore closer to Sharron's spirit. She sat in the spot, like her mother. She removed the remote control from the creased cushion, like her mother. And finally, she turned the TV onto the *BBC Morning News* on the queue of Anthony Eccleby thumping down the stairs. *Like Her Mother*.

"Morning, Bella," he yawned, entering the lounge archway wearing a black dressing gown. Underneath, black and red pyjama bottoms, navy blue slippers, and a plain pyjama top; all gifts from Sharron Rose when they spent their last Christmas together.

"Morning," she murmured, every letter pronounced clearly, though, but still as plain as every *morning* reply since ten years ago.

"Watching the news again like your mother, I see," Anthony stated, leaning against the curved wall.

"Yip." She turned and looked dead into her father's blue eyes. "I hope you're still coming with me to wish her a happy birthday, by the way."

Anthony quivered at the Sharron-look his daughter gave him.

"Y-Yeah, of course I am," he stuttered, deliberately turning his attention to the TV.

Stretching *the truth*.

"In other news..." Steven started, sitting next to his co-host in the studio, clearly reading from a script as he spoke statically. Behind them, less important news popped up on a magnificent LED screen. Anthony inched closer to the couch, where the remote sat. This particular story lured the sixteen-year-old in, too, making her unconscious of the opportunity that arose on her father. "Local police have yet to confirm the abrupt death of Castlehead's favourite daughter, Sharron Rose. However, Chief Pattison has allowed us to announce that the force suspect that Sharron's death wasn't an accident, and that she had been..."

Anthony swiftly cut off the television by swooping up the clicker, unintentionally prompting Isabella to stand up and send her into a fit of disappointment, yet she had no time to object to his actions as Anthony sent her upstairs immediately to get ready for her visit with Sharron.

He exhaled relief. But it had been an extremely long time since the thought of what had happened that night crossed his mind, almost forcing it to slip away as the years passed.

4: THEN

The Rose-Eccleby family parked up at the Jaxson Bay car park on *that* day after Isabella had her last nightmare for a decade.

But it was quite a while before she would be trembling in her bed. For now, Isabella was more bothered about making the largest sandcastle with her mother rather than having a scarring nightmare with her father trying to calm her down.

The sky was blue. *Bluer than usual*, Sharron thought. Even if it wasn't possible, it was true to her. Not a cloud in the sky, but the coastal wind was ferocious; shaking the cars of chilling citizens, causing grains of sand to rise up like they were forming a sandstorm, even causing a beefy man to tumble off his chair and spill his ice-cold Foster's beer all over his sweating, hairy chest. But still, *that* sky. And under it, a never-ending crystal bed of water called the North Sea. Exiting their Mercedes Benz, Sharron leaned against the open door in front of her and gazed at the majestic ocean that spoke to the people on shore with every splashing wave, urging them to go out and have a paddle. Sharron would most definitely be having a paddle in the bone-chilling water when she had the chance, but Isabella only would if she had to.

Forced, more like.

Although a huge fan of the beach, Isabella was never fond of water, especially the water in the pool of Laworth Leisure Centre.

It was the first and last time they went swimming as a family. Laworth Leisure Centre, a ten-minute drive, consisted of two floors – the ground for the pool area, and upstairs for the gym – bringing soloists and families together for a fun-filled day out.

She was five going on six the first time she swam, wearing a bathing suit of star-shaped sea shells, pink, yellow, and blue; the same bathing suit she would wear at the beach. And to go with the suit, armbands of one of her favourite television characters, *Shelly*.

This leisure centre trip was at a time when you could say Sharron was actually mentally stable enough to know what she was doing, being the parent to try to teach her daughter how to swim.

It's okay, Mammy's here, is what Sharron would say when Isabella thought she was drowning and not swimming correctly, with Anthony minding his own business, not paying any attention when sitting in the centre's glass fronted cafe. Yet, it was what happened an hour into the session that shook the young Isabella.

She was standing on the edge of the pool, looking down at what looked like the depths of the ocean. Such a small girl. Her hands clasped in front of her, twiddling, feeling much lighter without her armbands on dragging her down when she walked, but kept her up in the water. She couldn't contain her excitement when she found out ten minutes prior that she would be attending swimming lessons at the start of the new term, more eager than ever to get into the deep end when she reached level five; only for an unknown figure to shove her into the dark pit which she couldn't escape from, the sides of the pool closing in along with the grip of a ghostly hand trying to drag her down to Hell.

Even outside of Wardle Gardens, darkness enclosed and made her feel trapped forever – for both the mother and the daughter.

Since then, Isabella went nowhere near water unless it was shallow and reached her ankles.

Isabella Rose-Eccleby was vulnerable. She was protected. She was small for a six-year-old. Her sunny hair reached her back, almost to her backside, resembling one of her heroes, Rapunzel. Like Rapunzel, Bella had green luminescent eyes that shone in whatever light she stood under. A small, pointy nose, sharp eyebrows, pink cheeks, and rosy-red lips – even without lipstick – formed her face. Anthony always said that Isabella was her mother's daughter. As for Sharron, she did have those sharp eyebrows, and those emerald eyes, the same bright lips that lured her husband in for a kiss whenever she desired, and finally, short, wine red hair. Isabella's mannerisms were just like her father's, though; the way she spoke, the way she walked, the way she always wanted to make people proud, and especially the way she cheerfully flung her hands around when she told a story to her parents at a time when they would be settling down for the night.

They all stood at the car when they first hopped out, allowing the cool breeze to relax them, and letting the sight of the North Sea draw them in with the soothing sound of the waves crashing into the cliffs high aside the beach and overflowing the rock pools.

"Come on, let's go!" cheered Sharron, only to Isabella, running off and teasing her daughter to catch her in the soft sand.

"Okay..." Anthony laughed breathlessly at his wife and child starting the fun without him. "I guess I'll be getting the stuff then," he moaned to himself, accepting the challenge of carrying everything down to shore.

It was when the tide started to go out when Anthony finally made it down the stone footsteps to the beach itself, struggling to carry everything and even resulting in him kicking his own bag down the steps like a football. Sharron and Isabella's bags were hooked under both his arms like a pair of rugby balls, and in the clutches of his hands were the bags of refreshments, snacks, and beach toys.

Anthony dropped the bags carelessly on the sand at the back of the beach, puffing and panting where the small huts stood in rainbow colour order. After catching his breath and overseeing his family having the best time they've had in a long time, he laid out the towels for all three of them, happily lying there with one of his cans of Bud, smiling and loving life on his own.

She seems alright so far, he thought, dozing off into a sleep that wasn't as deep as to say that he didn't know where he was, but a sleep in which he could still sense his surroundings.

His sleep only lasted about fifteen minutes as Isabella and Sharron wanted Anthony to join the fun, too, deciding to sneakily pinch a bucket from one of the bags, and without making a sound there and back, Isabella filled the bucket with the bitter ocean water, and made the decision to tip the raw liquid onto his balding head.

Anthony awakened instantly, shocked to see Isabella and Sharron rolling around in the sand, laughing hysterically like a pair of hyenas. But their laughing came to an immediate halt when Anthony stood up like a monster rising from the dead, jokily threatening to chuck his prey into the sea. They ran for their lives as Beasty Boy Eccleby chased them into the shallow waters.

Only to their ankles.

"I'm goin' to gobble you both up for my supper," Anthony roared joyfully, splashing his family with little waves of water.

With all the commotion getting the better of Anthony, the family learned that nobody would match the willpower of Isabella Rose-Eccleby as she took down the monster, and pounded him with soft shots to the stomach; all of them laughing as they played, not wanting the moment to end.

It would end for Sharron.

Sharron laughed, but then stopped. She froze, her eyes fixing onto the cliff at the far end of the beach. She held in a gasp of fear, still quite observant and aware of her whereabouts; unlike what happened the night before. And with Anthony and Isabella just starting to comprehend that Sharron left the moment, they stopped too.

Oh, no, Anthony thought, acting instantly on the situation that arose.

And with Anthony starting to rise up and attempting to snap Sharron out of whatever she was in, that moment was lost – the moment that made them a family. Sharron turned ninety degrees, staring out at the vast ocean meeting with the sky at the horizon. It called to her.

One step, two steps, three steps, four. Five steps, six steps, seven steps, more.

Into the sea Sharron went, getting her sunflower dress soaked by the salty sea. The further she went, the more she descended, her mind elsewhere, but still with the goal to reach as far as she could to the horizon until she couldn't walk no more.

That was it. That was all Isabella could remember. It's been just over a decade since that day; the last memory Isabella could recall having fun. There were memories of old which she couldn't remember as a whole, locked away in the secured chest that she wasn't able to find the key to. She grew up but didn't move on. And now, how time had flown since that point, a point when she despised the fact that she was going to see her mother's resting place.

5: NOW

Isabella was fully freshened up, making sure to look presentable for her mother. She stood upright in her bedroom, looking herself in the eyes through a long, rectangular mirror that was supposed to hang up on the wall, but leaned against it instead.

"Come on, Isabella!" Anthony's deep, posh voice was heard from the bottom of the stairs. Very Received Pronunciation, every letter said within each word. "You're going to be late, and you *do* remember how impatient your mother got." Anthony checked his Apple Watch on his right wrist, reading 9:45. In fact, *he* wasn't even ready, still in his loungewear.

"Two seconds, Anthony!" she replied from her room, with a sense of irritation from her father rushing her. "I'm just finishing off my makeup!"

And she was doing just that, not stretching the truth like her father. She made her red lips even redder with the brightest of lipsticks, and some bronzer to make her cheeks pop. That was all she would put on for her mother. Isabella was the same since six, but reaching 5 feet 8 inches at fifteen, and cutting her hair to shoulder-length, with a voice of a wealthy angel. The voice of this angel, though, could go if she was in a mood. Sharron was the same. First, the look with their eyebrows pointed down sharply at their noses like arrows, then the face would scrunch up, and finally, not a voice of an angel, but a voice of an old woman screeching through a megaphone who criticised everything she saw from her window. But in Isabella and Sharron's case, they would criticise Anthony for doing a wrong. In addition to that, the passing of Sharron just made her temper worse... only when Anthony took it like a dog being tortured by a dog whistle.

"How many times do I have to tell you? Do NOT call me *Anthony*. I'm your DAD. D-A-D. Dad!" he roared with a grunt afterwards.

Isabella opened then slammed the door behind her, more signs of frustration. She strutted down the staircase like a model that wore a knee-length skirt over skin-tight leggings, an ironed white polo, a smart jacket that went to her waist, and the flattest of shoes. Her hair was tied back in a ponytail so her hair wouldn't dance wildly into a mad scientist's style in the North-Eastern wind.

It was said that a storm was invading the UK soon. The storm would be floating in from the West, skimming through Northern Ireland, completely surpassing Wales, the Republic, and most of Scotland, aiming directly for Castlehead and the North-East. Many storms have hit the UK prior to this day, but none would leave such an impact on Isabella like the one that was yet to come.

"Sorry, *Dad*," said Isabella arrogantly, now face-to-face with Anthony at the bottom of the stairs as if they were ready to rage war against one another. There was tension, and the tension flooded Chessington Close. But it started to die down when Isabella asked as calmly as she could, noticing that he wasn't changed: "Why are you not ready? I thought you were coming, too."

Anthony didn't have the courage to rejoinder, uncomfortably resisting the temptation to look into the evil eyes that Bella started to gaze at him, her look like a mind control device. Look into them and she got her way.

"I'm so, so, sorry," he finally burst out, his voice breaking in fear, apologetic.

Bella boiled up with both rage and heartbreak, feeling betrayed *again* by Anthony. It was as if she was being stabbed in the back by a thousand knives, although this wasn't the first time he had chickened out of doing something involving his dead wife, so deep down, Isabella didn't know why she was as surprised as she was.

"But it's her birthday," she clarified, admonishing Anthony for his decision. "And you lied."

"I didn't lie. No." said Anthony, denying his obvious fib, his daughter throwing her finger ruthlessly at him, making her father feel like he had hit an all-time low by *stretching the truth*.

"You did. You did. You Did. You Did. YOU DID. YOU DID. YOU DID!"

"ENOUGH!" Anthony laid down the law, shattering the windows as his voice echoed through the Chessington Close halls, just like how he had shattered Isabella's heart. He wasn't going to stand for anyone who called him a liar and rub it in. It was like two rabid animals clawing at each other's insides, hitting each other where it hurts. "I Just Can't Make It."

There was another moment of silence, the tension brewing over the entirety of Chess Street now. Not making eye contact, the father and daughter knew if they did, shit would hit the fan even more. And without saying a word, leaving Isabella to whimper like a puppy, Anthony revealed a bouquet of Sharron's favourite flowers from the kitchen, roses. Again, not saying a word, Anthony handed Isabella the bouquet peacefully. Both thinking alike, Isabella did what Anthony had expected from her: she said nothing, took the flowers, grateful for the gesture, and left without a fuss, leaving Anthony alone with his thoughts.

The front double doors didn't slam shut. They barely even shut on Isabella's accord. Anthony had to shut them properly; so soft that he didn't hear them click together. All he could do now was to sit in the lounge, on his side of the couch, exhale relief that the episode was finally over, but sigh in absolute guilt, causing the thought of all three of them together as a family unbearable.

Sharron Rose had been dead for ten years, but Anthony still had trouble putting the pieces back together,

He rubbed his eyes desperately, hoping to snooze, but the sweet sound of Sharron's voice replaying in his head stopped him. *You could've gone for her*, he could hear, as if she was right behind him, standing there, hand on his shoulder, softly rubbing it, relaxing him.

You could've gone for her.

He could've gone for her, yes, but he didn't. It was back when Sharron was alive and well, whenever Isabella and Sharron would do something that was important, she would advise her husband that if he wasn't going to come for her, come for his daughter. It was his life he was missing out on, and in the back of her mind, Sharron knew that if this kept continuing, Anthony wasn't going to have a daughter.

Anthony Eccleby always said that he listened to his wife's advice, and honestly, he did at points, but only for a certain amount of time like a slimy frog leaping from one lily pad to the next in a matter of seconds; one day, the advice would be stuck in his mind, the next, said advice would hop right out.

6

She sat there weeping in front of her mother's grave, on the bench dedicated to Sharron's spirit.

An oak wood bench, smooth, six years old, but still felt brand new, the idea came to Isabella when she was ten and Anthony loved it when it was first considered. Bella didn't just see it as a bench to commemorate the best mother in the world, she thought of it as a place to reflect – not just on her mother – the memories that *weren't* locked away in the chest with the lost key, and if she just wanted to be alone, feeling closer to her mother.

Isabella never did know how Sharron truly died.

She sat there, still weeping uncontrollably, head cupped in her hands, looking down at the flat black shoes she wore for the occasion. It wasn't the correct clothing for the misty, overcast, Castlehead weather, but she didn't care, thinking about what would've made her mother proud. And knowing that Sharron would've screamed the house down because Anthony – apparently – was unable to make it, it didn't make her upset, but laugh instead as she knew in her right mind that he deserved it.

Having trouble wiping away the countless tears racing down her face, she listened out for Rose to say something to comfort her.

Don't cry, darling. Isabella felt her mother's presence behind her, feeling warm in the cold for the first time in a long time.

"Don't cry, darling."

That time, it sounded more real – less like her mother. With a glimpse of sunlight peeking through the black and grey clouds like it was spying on the sixteen-year-old, Bella noticed a tall shadow lurking behind her like an undead soul. She looked at the shadow, not upwards – yet.

Whoever was there, though, looked awfully familiar.

Whoever was there was eager to talk to Isabella Rose-Eccleby.

Whoever was there was NOT her mother.

Chapter Two

Strike I – Tony Lesterson

1

The figure didn't budge, nor did Isabella, who still sat head down on her mother's bench sobbing. But whoever the figure was that prowled behind her wasn't the ghost of her mother.

They were taller and more masculine, more masculine than her father. And Bella was only taking notes from the shadow she looked at pasted on the ground. The longer the figure stood, the more uncomfortable the girl became.

"It's okay, darling," the figure said again, leaning in towards her, causing her to scoot further along the bench. "Don't worry, I'm here."

Isabella finally glanced up to see a man among men. He was buff and rough. His hidden eyes gazed at her, face covered by a hood. He smelled of cigarettes and alcohol – a smell that lured Bella in just a touch.

"Thank you, I guess," she mumbled under her breath, more confidently looking up at the man, not a boy.

He circled around the bench, Isabella scooching away to the other side of the bench to allow him to sit. It was terribly uncomfortable that a man a good number of years older than her sat there gently smiling, hoping for a smile back. For now, anyone but her father was who she needed to feel loved. However, it wasn't until he got a good look of her face that he noticed she was still wrongly letting tears flow down her cheeks.

"Don't cry, don't cry." The man leaned in amorously, wiping away the tears that damaged her face. "Don't let those tears ruin this gorgeous face."

Holding back the tears as best as she could, Isabella blushed, almost forgetting where she was and the reason why she was there.

The man came in from out of nowhere like a bolt of lightning, making his presence known. His voice thunderous like the roar of a lion, echoing throughout Central Cemetery. His eyes were blue as shining sapphires that lured in his victims, sending them into a sense of vulnerability. Spikes of prickly brown hair ran down the side of his face to his chin, moving upwards around his lips faintly, and below his bottom lip was a clear stitched scar oozing with blood and puss fiercely wanting to burst out.

And that was when Isabella turned ninety degrees to stare at Sharron's grave, in cannon with the newly met lad who noticed a second afterwards.

"Ah, *Sharron Rose*," he read aloud, only for Isabella to give a look to not to, so he continued reading in his head:

IN LOVING MEMORY OF SHARRON ROSE

DATE OF BIRTH - 5th MARCH, 1979

DATE OF DEATH - 6th MARCH, 2009

They sat there silently, with the man most eager to continue on with the graceful greeting. Two pairs of couples past along the pathway heading up to Central Church rudely eyeing the seated pair – a gay couple and a couple of Indian descent.

"Don't look at them," she murmured, embarrassed.

"Fucking hypocrites," he snarled, with a gobsmacked Isabella gasping at her first hearing of a curse word. "They shouldn't be allowed in this town," he muttered. But knowing Isabella wanted to change the subject, the man changed his tone. "This your mother?" he asked softly, pointing unclearly. Isabella nodded. "I bet she was a great mother."

"Oh, she was," she finally replied with no mumble or murmur.

He smiled proudly, like he had just ticked something off a checklist of things to talk about. And now, he thought it was time to make his move.

"So, listen..."

"Sugar-Honey-Iced-Tea," Isabella burst out without warning, rising up after a finger-tip touched the far side of her shoulder.

"What's wrong?" asked the man, reacting with a leap of faith off the bench, with Isabella noticing he was a beanstalk compared to her miniature stature.

"I've got to go now." It was difficult to understand what she had said. She rushed off passed him to the side exit of Central Cemetery onto St Christopher Road.

Right idea, Isabella heard her mother say... but ignored it as best as she could.

Leaving the man alone at the bench, the guilt started to creep in as – as much as she wouldn't want to admit it – there was actually something about this guy;

although he appeared to experience a poor life, he knew the world, yet also having a certain charm.

As if he already knew Isabella's next move, the man jumped with glee, trying to keep his cool, when she turned back to him to apologise for the inconvenience she may have caused. Telling her not to worry, the man mostly paid no attention to what she was babbling on about – something about her mother – and focused on her glowing face and radiant body.

And just then, suddenly, with as much confidence as he could muster, without restraining himself from rejection, just as Isabella turned once again to head out onto St Christopher Road, the man asked, "How about your number?"

She stopped still in her tracks.

Don't do it, Isabella.

The surprised teenager looked back, in the middle of a life changing decision. Should she, or should she not?

"Sure," she said, not needing to think about it and shrugging her previous thought of a life *changing decision* off.

He strutted like a peacock to her, showing off all his beautifully patterned feathers. A cheesy smirk ran across his face, but Isabella thought more about what was on the inside, for true beauty is found within.

That is not always the case.

They exchanged numbers like how Year Three children would exchange names on the school playground, gleefully: not a care in the world. Not a care in the world for her father, not a care in the world herself. And not a care in the world for her mother – the initial reason why she was there in the first place. It had obviously slipped out of her mind.

His name was Tony Lesterson, number written in Isabella's contact list on her phone – top of the list. They walked out together and chatted about talking later on that night, and even meeting up at some point. Tony didn't go as far as to hug the vulnerable girl at the Central Cemetery gate, but politely shook her hand for longer than three seconds. After the grip was released, they went their separate ways; one down St Christopher Road heading down to the junction of said road and Liberty Street, the other up the road to Castlehead Station-- a terminal for both local and national rail services.

Strike One, Isabella. Remember, three strikes and you're out.

The rule was introduced to Isabella when she was around toddler age, and for some reason stuck with her for her whole life. Sharron would use it in any scenario, whether that be as small as breaking a glass, or as big as getting Tony Lesterson's number. Fortunately for Bella, she had never actually reached strike three before, because if she did, it was the end – not figuratively... realistically.

2

It was a late quarter after three when Isabella had returned home to Chessington Close, although she did almost get off at Fellmarsh Station to walk up to Wardle Gardens – *her true home*, she thought (knew).

Anthony awaited on his daughter's return, tapping his foot to the beat of a new song on the radio, arms crossed, more disappointed than angry – a bad impression of an angry Sharron.

The temptation to snigger at her father's scrunched up pug face was lost when the music stopped, it was like they had restarted where they left off – a bit more soft toned, this time though. Anthony gathered that neither of them couldn't handle a screaming match once again, so he relaxed his arms, showed a face of no emotion, and gently started to communicate with his daughter.

"Where were you?" he asked firmly, watching Isabella slowly walk past him to stand on the bottom step.

"I went to see Mother," she replied, hoping he didn't notice the time.

"What? Five hours ago?"

Isabella thought for a believable excuse.

"I bumped into Jess and Hannah on my way back," she responded with a heavy heart of guilt.

Anthony looked at her, realising that she wasn't looking back, desperate to go up the stairs to her room and just be with her thoughts. However, that's not what Anthony truly wanted; he wanted to talk and apologise and forget what had happened that morning, hoping to rejoice.

"Oh, right," he said with slight suspicion, hesitant to ask further questions as if he was scared of a continuation of this morning's argument. Lucky enough, she had instantly replied with a convincing story.

"Yeah. I left from the St Christopher exit of the cemetery, and started walking up to the station, as I do, and that's when I started getting peckish for food. So, you know that Tesco on St James' Road next to Castlehead Station?" She didn't allow him to reply, as if thinking that he knew the place. "Of course you do," she continued. "And I went in, bought myself some treats for later – I didn't forget, Dad – and now, here I am."

Isabella started up the stairs, wanting no contact with anyone apart from the authentic dolls in her room until she would go down to her father and watch a series of their favourite films.

It was a sort of tradition every year on this day for Isabella – sometimes her dad, too – to visit Mother for half an hour to an hour, head off to Tesco for treats, then home for a pyjama afternoon on the couch with a bowl of snacks on the mat in front of them, both father and daughter all snuggled up on their respective sides of the couch, along with three consecutive films --Sharron's most enjoyed films – on the TV.

All this done before a quarter after three.

With Isabella now in Sharron's corner of the couch, Sharron's spirit played as a bridge in the middle, hoping their communication stayed strong and wouldn't collapse.

But the one thing that had caught Anthony off-guard when Bella had been telling her cogent story was that she didn't even reference her two best friends, Hannah, and Jess, but he was unable to catch her out as she headed up the stairs.

3

Strike One, Isabella.

"Remember, three strikes and you're out," Isabella repeated to herself as she left Central Cemetery, walking up the road as newly met Tony Lesterson walked in the opposite direction. That wasn't their first and only encounter that day.

She walked with a hop and skip in her step and an unadmitted smile on her face as she headed up towards the train terminal, Castlehead Station. Despite her meeting with Tony, Bella was still precisely on schedule. Her next step was to head into Tesco for her bags of treats for later on.

Although she was hoping that she and Anthony could reconcile once she was home, that was in the back of her mind. The thought of Tony Lesterson kept creeping up bang in the front. She kept getting caught off guard and misdirected herself as, at the junction, she turned onto Liberty Street instead of continuing onward.

Isabella grunted at herself for that obvious mistake, and had to cut through an alleyway between the back of the Tesco and a rival store aside it.

By this time, the sun had managed to break through the stormy clouds and let out rays of yellow and pieces of the sky, but it had felt like day turned into night in a matter of seconds as once she entered the alley, the monstrous buildings blocked the sun and overshadowed the surrounding car parks, local shops, and Castlehead Station.

The alley was narrow. A tight squeeze and compressed enough for people with claustrophobia to break into utter madness, Isabella was able to stretch her arms out and reach both buildings. Kicking the litter to the side with each stride, she came across graffiti on both walls; some of names, some of inspiring quotes, but also some quite disturbing.

"*She broke into the house at night, nobody around,*" she read. "*She felt like there was nothing left for her in the world to live for.*" She continued reading in her head until she couldn't read anymore. Too sad. But the last sentence caught her attention, and caused her to blurt it out loud. "*All will be revealed soon... Isabella.*"

"Excuse me, Miss?"

Two detectives of the Castlehead Criminal Investigation Department grabbed her attention. She turned to them and couldn't explain what she had just read. She looked back at the green graffiti and all it read was: *You only have one life, you decide how to live it.*

"Erm..." She shook her head. "Sorry, I must've been talking to myself."

The officers looked at each other simultaneously with the same reaction on their faces, cringing and amusement.

"You shouldn't be in this alley on your own, Miss," the smaller officer clarified.

"Oh, sorry," she said with realisation. "I was just cutting through." She clearly meant no harm to whatever two detectives were doing in the alley, too. Worry spread across her face, thinking she was going to be taken away or something.

"Don't worry," the larger and broader officer suggested. "We're just on an investigation into the murders of a number of girls who were out late last night. Screams were heard from around this area," he explained.

"Okay. Sorry for the inconvenience."

"No harm done, we'll just advise you to be around this area in a group next time. Clear?"

"Crystal," she agreed, her legs twitching, ready to leg it to Tesco.

She was surprised that she was able to make it past the officers and out of the alley without being brutally abused, or something worse. Isabella caught her breath, puffing and panting as she looked up at the big bold red letters on top of the building, reading *Tesco.*

The automatic doors opened wide as she, and a bunch of random pedestrians, entered, all with a goal to find what they wanted to purchase.

Two rows of ten and ten columns of two spread across the popular supermarket, all presenting different products, whether that be clothes, frozen foods, spices, or snacks, Tesco had it. For anyone who hadn't visited this Tesco before – or any Tesco, for that matter – it would be like a hunt for treasure; you would need a map, and when 'X' marked the spot, that's the aisle you would venture to. The trolleys were the ships and the shoppers were the sailors, off on a voyage across the Tesco seas. As for Isabella, who was still at the entrance/shore, she was able to tame the sea as she knew exactly where she was heading; up past the row of many old-fashioned tills and around to aisle number ten where the crisps, sweets, and chocolate were.

In the process of completing her last voyage down from the snacks and drinks aisle down to the tills, she took a detour as she had come to perceive a familiar stature stacking the dairy aisle, aisle number six.

She had hoped that her wide eyes had deceived her, looming over the figure stacking the red capped milk and blue capped milk beside one another, not caring about the order in which they had to go in.

"Tony?" she blurted as if she didn't intentionally ask.

The man turned, and it was Tony.

"Isabella!" he exclaimed, astonished, spilling a carton of milk on the floor. "Wh...What are you doin' here?" he asked Isabella, acting like she had done something wrong, acting like she shouldn't have been seen with him.

"I didn't know you worked here," said Bella.

Tony hesitated to admit it.

"Ah, yes. Yes I do." He quickly added: "But this isn't a full-time thing, it's just to pass me by, you know." Isabella smiled innocently, nodding. "I'll be back in a sec." Tony rushed off to gather a mop and bucket to clean the mess caused by the startled adult. He returned with the mop under his arm and bucket tightly in his grasp. "What you doin' here, then?" he asked again, this time in a much calmer tone.

"I just bought some snacks for home, that's all," she explained.

"Oh, right."

Tony focused on shining the floor up real nice before he continued the current conversation with Isabella, who just stood there waiting patiently. After a couple of minutes, Tony had finally plopped the soaked mop in the red bucket of filthy water, leaning the wooden handle against the shelf steadily.

"So..." Isabella huffed.

"So..." echoed Tony awkwardly, but followed up swiftly: "I get off work in about fifteen minutes, and I was just thinking if you waited... we could like head out for a bit?"

She didn't reply immediately, signifying to him that she might reject him for what she originally had planned. *If this lass blows me off for her bitchy mates, then I know she's not worth my time*, he thought, imagining her friends being stuck-up and annoying.

"I don't know," she said uncomfortably, at first, letting him off easy. "It's just that my dad would be wondering where I am."

"Look, we'll be back before you know it," he pleaded, imploring her to accept.

He jokily pouted, his droopy bottom lip making her let out a little giggle. And knowing he had persuaded her, he laughed along, eager to jump with glee when she did want to go (to get) with him.

4

Isabella didn't say a word to Anthony during their late film watching, barely even touching the snacks she had purchased for the occasion. A pile of Sharron's favourite films stood high on the stand which the vase of roses was on. Not one of them was touched until Anthony had finally spoken up and asked why a film wasn't on. Back in the day, Isabella would have a film ready to play even before they had changed into their bedclothes.

"Yeah, sorry, just my friends," she replied unconvincingly, her eyes fixed on her phone, tapping away every five seconds.

"Hannah and Jess?"

"If you say so," she said to herself, nodding slightly as if she was actually paying attention.

Anthony didn't reply, just managing to make out what she had just said, because he knew far too well that her best friends, Hannah, and Jess, never disturbed her on this day during their film time.

Even during the entire duration of the first and only film they had stuck on, Isabella's eyes were locked on her phone. It's dinging constantly got under Anthony's skin, but Bella did switch the phone to silent. The buzzing wasn't any better. With every funny moment from the movie came a bellowing laugh from both Father and Daughter – but for different reasons. At the points of laughter, Anthony wiped away the tears of laughter, and Isabella hid her red, blushing face.

And once the film had concluded after the eight-minute credits, Isabella legged it upstairs to her room, slamming the door behind her, so Anthony wouldn't be able to hear the flirtatious conversation being said that came from both sides of the call.

"I guess I'm putting away the DVDs," Anthony assumed.

Regular *oooo*'s and laughter continued throughout the night, disturbing Anthony's slumber. There was a point when Anthony couldn't take it, 1:57 that night and Anthony stormed out of his bedroom, in tight boxer briefs and a white vest, and nearly ripped Isabella's door off its hinges.

"Do you realise what time it is?" he rhetorically questioned his daughter, hiding her phone from her dad – still on – and sitting innocently at the foot of her bed. Isabella didn't reply, more focused on how Anthony's balding head of hair stuck out like a mad scientist's, bags under his eyes, even his bags had bags.

All through the stalemate between the two family members, Isabella's gut was spinning with butterflies, with the phone still on, on speaker, she had wished that Anthony couldn't hear Tony Lesterson's blabbering mouth in between her legs.

Bella looked apologetically at her father. He sighed and recalled what had happened that morning. He dropped his head and shook as she calmly shut the door, leaving his daughter to go back to speaking to the man.

Anthony leaned his face to the door, overhearing his daughter's conversation.

"You could've gotten me in a heap of trouble," he heard her whisper with a laugh.

"Sorry. I can't stop," he managed to make out. That time, not coming from Isabella. Although he made out what was said, lucky for Isabella, he couldn't make out that it was a bloke she was on the phone to, Tony's voice breaking through the door and breaking up on the phone.

Alright, stop now, he heard next to him. He imagined his loving wife standing next to him, arms folded and ashamed of him, although not sounding it.

"I just worry about her," he replied, turning, tip toeing back to his room, getting back into bed along with Sharron.

I know, she's growing up, she cooed, snuggling up with her husband in her woolly pj's. *You can't keep her 'Daddy's little girl' forever.*

"Yeah, I know. I know," he sighed, dozing off into a dream that he wouldn't remember the next day.

5

The night flew by, and the thought of school every morning would exhilarate her with excitement and joy, tempting her to get out of bed. But that morning, Isabella was dreading having to walk into class, slumped, arms swinging back and forth carelessly, and seeing her fellow students look at her astonished, wondering what had happened to the girl who, the week before, was in class half an hour before everyone else, but now half an hour late.

She collapsed onto her designated seat on table six, next to Hannah, the table in front of Jess, but the table behind Katherine Bates, her spider web hair – shooting off in all directions – restricting Isabella's view of both the whiteboard and the electronic board.

"Jeez, you look awful," acknowledged Jess, a reasonably sized girl with great round spectacles, blue eyes as bright as the sea, and lengthy strands of beeline honey hair.

"Thanks," Isabella said sarcastically, turning around revealing to Jess a bulldog face, snorting every second, her hair clammy and greasy. "That's what every girl wants to hear in the morning."

"No problem," chuckled Jess, not gathering the clear sarcasm.

Isabella turned back around to face Katherine's mad hair, and leaned in next to Hannah.

"How did she ever get into this school?" whispered Isabella.

"God knows," Hannah replied, her fruity voice overpowering Isabella's gentle voice, shrugging her broad shoulders, her lips always pouting after every word and whenever she didn't speak.

The three friends all fiddled with their hair during first period, normally it would be just Jess and Hannah, with Bella shushing them every five minutes and telling them to stop messing on. Today, Isabella joined in.

Mrs Burns went on to talk about the human body this and organism that; words that would commonly be in Isabella's dictionary, but most likely would have had to translate them during this dragging hour.

Their voices echoed through the packed halls of Castle Grange Sixth Form. The loudest of them all was Hannah's.

"So, what's going on with this lad you keep mentioning?" she asked, tying her bronze brown hair into a bun.

"Yeah, come on, tell us," Jess pleaded.

Isabella bit her lip and blushed.

"Oh, I... I don't know." She shrugged her shoulders, hiding her face, turning it away to quickly glance at the grey floor that harmonised with the green walls. "I think we're just friends."

The trio continued walking down to the end of the hall to a door which led to a stack of – what seemed like – endless stairs to the second floor.

Jess and Hannah rolled their eyes.

"Someone who you talk to all night isn't just a *friend*," Hannah stated mockingly. "So, just tell us. For Christ's sake, he can't be worse than Billy Curtsy."

And at that point, all the lasses remembered fond memories of primary school; their first kisses, boyfriends, and crushes, going off topic and onto memories of unforgettable childhood moments.

6

They stumbled through Chessington Close's front doors, unaware that there were neighbours, bellowing out laughter as on their way back, Hannah, Jess, and Isabella recalled Hannah's humiliation of a prom date that past July.

All the years of hard work paid off for all three of them when it came to their prom, which had been booked to be at Michael Manor – a house that hid within the hills that overlooked and surrounded Castlehead.

Many rumours had circulated throughout both primary and secondary school about Michael Manor; rumours about all the owners horrifically dying, rumours about the current owner's existence, but mostly about the house being haunted. Michael Manor stood by itself against its hills. Walls continued upright, even during the heaviest storms, as the worn bricks met neatly, stairs croaked without the placement of feet, floors were firm, and its doors kept darkness within. A darkness in which Wardle Gardens could've replicated.

Thomas Hill leavers, class of 2018, stood as still as statues when they were wowed by the great hall of Michael Manor. Candles hooked on the walls and disco lights – supported by electrical cables – hung from the ceiling around the golden light chandelier, allowing heavenly light into the hell house.

The group were given explicit instructions not to wander, a message given by the owner of the house; the only place the one hundred students could roam was the great hall, or the lavatory, but only if it was absolutely necessary. However, going to the toilet wasn't the three best friends' admiration; their true admiration was to make the most of the *best day of their lives* and party like animals, forgetting about all their dates not even twenty minutes in.

Billy Curtsy was there, too, but was on his own that night. Jess was asked by the school nerd, Samuel Evans. Hannah finally found the confidence to ask her crush of five years – the entire duration of secondary school – Xavier Benson. As for Isabella, she tagged along with

Jason James, a kid who she was friends with but didn't *like* – a last resort.

All three of them left their dates for the dance floor and girlfriends. The wooden floorboards of Michael Manor shuddered when all the remaining dancing students jumped in unison to the beats of many remixes. But by the end of the night, it was time for the couples dance to determine the Prom King and Queen. Only Hannah and Xavier were in the line for the throne out of the three pairs, impressing the judges for most of the dance until Xavier toppled it, smacking his face off the ground when they ran for each other, meeting in the middle. They all laughed it off during the after party at Jason's – a clean party without any interaction with drink or drugs. Isabella had only stayed for an hour at the after party, feeling twinges down her spine with Jason edging uncomfortably close to her as the night concluded.

7

That very same twinge returned to tease Isabella's spine whenever Hannah and Jess derisively brought up the man that they hadn't heard much of yet. They giggled through the passing day and made a pact that Isabella shall tell them of Tony Lesterson when Hannah and Jess returned for the slumber party on Saturday night.

Not only did the twinge tingle Bella's spine when Tony was mentioned but that very night whilst she had laid there, motionless, glaring up at the ceiling, she moved like a snake trying to release the pain shooting through her spine. It was the fuss that made her head hit the pillow, then she was out like a light.

8

I am home, she thought. And stopped and trembled at the thought of how she ended up from her Chessington Close bed to Wardle Gardens' front step. She knocked, and then BANG. *Isabella jumped back out of fright, but then reached out for the faded doorknob, there was no ear-aching bang, but a gentle creak of the black door and the echo of the reveal to a front passage that was merely a collection of worn out bricks, cement, and glass. To Isabella, though, it was a newly built passage with shiny wood flooring, white painted walls, and stairs carpeted with the softest material. The junction at the top of the stairs spit off to either a collection of bedrooms or a bathroom. One step, two steps, three steps, four. Five steps, six steps, seven steps, and more. Isabella toured around the house with the urge to find her family who were in the lounge, the heart of the house; the Rose-Eccleby family were the organisms and the rooms were the bones. Gleefully hopping down each step like a six-year-old, her heart pounded with trepidation, and knocked on the door tunefully asking for the attention of her mother and father – especially her mother. No reply. However, a scream of pain came from the lounge.*

"I had to take one of you," she heard a witchy voice coo.

A mournful cry came from the lounge, and in unison, a cry of hope came from the dreaming girl.

9

A screaming Isabella smacked her head against the headboard of her bed, weeping and alerting Anthony.

He burst in, reaching out to give comfort to who appeared to be the six-year-old who had a similarly traumatic nightmare close to ten years ago.

"It felt so real," she cried, breathing hysterically, clutching the edges of her mattress for dear life as if she was on the verge of falling from a height and which she saved herself from by holding onto the nearest object.

"I know, I know," her dad replied soothingly, rubbing her back softly.

He didn't need to talk to calm her; all he needed to do was just be there for his daughter.

God, the nightmare felt awfully familiar, like a follow up to a previous nightmare. Although exhaling fear and inhaling relief at a now constant rate, in the back of her mind, Isabella was trying to gather her thoughts and put two and two together, however, vaguely remembering the anamnesis of her haunted dreams, it wasn't as simple as a straightforward maths equation.

He babbled on, on about how nightmares can feel so real sometimes. He went on to explain how some nightmares can be worse than others; some may be as little as just the feeling that you're falling from a great height, others more significant and may have deeper meaning.

"Can you have a continuation of a nightmare you had previously?" she asked, seemingly out of the blue.

"Highly unlikely," he answered. Gathering that his daughter just might be settling down at this point, he rose and went for the door, but then froze. "Why ask?" he followed up, turning back to Isabella.

"I don't know. Just seemed familiar," she sniffed, yawning.

She never did tell Anthony, or Sharron for that matter, in great detail about her recurring nightmares way back when she was a child, nor would she have ever dreamed of doing so. *They would think I'm crazy*, she would think as she shivered, sobbing herself back to sleep. Even at sixteen, she never brought it up that she would see people at the foot of her bed, reaching out for her, dragging the duvet off her bed to clutch her feet and drag her away from where she felt most safe, not even at sixteen did she want to mention that her nightmares that she had at six began on the night of her grandmother's passing; the nightmare on that night only being a slight jump scare that didn't alarm her parents.

All this recollection of her and these nightmares raced through her brain as Anthony stood there for what seemed like ages, repeatedly asking if she was okay to head back off to her slumber.

"Bella? Bella? Bella? Bella?"

It was on the fourth *Bella* which snapped Isabella out of her thoughts.

"What?" she snapped. Anthony winced.

"Do you remember what nightmares do?" he asked, expecting the answer he received every time.

"Oh, my God." She rolled her eyes. "I know. I'm not six." Anthony gulped. "Now, let me go to bed, Anthony."

It was as if something had snapped and awakened a monster which couldn't be contained until Isabella got what she wanted. She calmed down, and repositioned herself back into bed once Anthony viciously slammed the door behind him.

With guilt already starting to stir in her body, all Isabella could do now was just think about how she could just snap at her father like that, knowing she had never done it beforehand, all while tackling the task of returning to sleep with all this fixed in her mind.

Chapter Three

First Dates

1

It was the Saturday of the long-awaited slumber party for Hannah, Jess, and Isabella – but Tony Lesterson didn't know that.

Rising early that morning, formulating a plan and schedule in his mind, Tony pottered around his house – which his dad actually owned, although Tony claimed that he bought it from his father – wondering what the next step in his *relationship* with Isabella was going to be.

As for Isabella, she planned out the night that she would host for her friends. It was a regular thing to have a slumber party once a month, taking turns each month, and they didn't like to admit it but it was a competition to see whether or not they could one-up each other.

Before arranging to meet with his cronies, Harvey and Jamie, Tony had spent the morning in his shaggy bottoms and stained vest, revealing cuts and bruises on his arms; cuts and bruises that weren't created by the self-harm he would gladly endure during low points in his life, but by the harm caused by a sick, twisted pile of rotting flesh with less and less willpower to continue on with every passing day.

"Here's your medicine, Da'," said Tony, offering a tub of – said to be – prescription pills to his father who the previous night had collapsed on the front step after hitting up every local bar in and around the Carson Estate. With no help from the lower-class region of Castlehead, Tony had no choice but to literally drag his father's weakened body and fold him up onto the couch, leaving him to rest and forget everything that had happened that night.

This had gone on since Tony's mother escaped.

The man had yet to respond, having no clue of his whereabouts, tossing, and turning whilst unaware that his son was there. He was close to rolling onto the coffee table laid out in between the 1980s style television and the torn couch, which when sat upon would let off a gust of dust, smoke, and even ash. Tony had saved his dad from rolling onto the table with cigarettes, broken glass, empty and smashed beer bottles, and even joints spread across it. Tony glanced down at the small, rectangular table and spotted a small cereal bowl. It was full, full of white tablets.

Tony sighed at the sight. *He must have thought about just saying that he took the pills*, Tony thought, taking away the bowl and placing it in the full kitchen sink on the other side of his home.

With tears in the carpet, Tony repeatedly tripped over each loose piece of carpet as he paced back and forth between sections of his home, clearing away all the beer bottles, unused medication, and everything else that Tony could use to sway Isabella into doing as he pleased.

If the drugs weren't going to kill him, then the alcohol, without a doubt, would.

2

Isabella stood there, waiting impatiently for Jess and Hannah to stop 'faffing around'. She stood there at the small wooden gate, it's wood wearing away, her fingers tapping on the fence as every second passed.

The front door slowly opened wide to reveal two teenage girls who acted like a pair of five-year-olds as they raced towards their best friend. Jess athletically leaped over the waist-height gate and pounced onto Isabella who received a shock, but knew it was all fun and games.

They had agreed to always meet up in the early hours of the afternoon whenever one of their annual slumber parties took place, getting the most time out of the day with each other.

The trio hopped and skipped through the dark alleys and uneasy streets, shining a little happiness in the rough neighbourhoods. Isabella led the way through an alleyway that ended with a junction, either left or right. It was at this point when all of them – even Jess – had gathered that they may have been messing about too much, paying no attention to their direction. Isabella chanced it and took a right, heading into the outskirts of the Carson Estate.

3

Carson Park – more like *Carson Dump* – was where Tony and his cronies were, laid back on a bench, pupils noticeably larger, and their heads hanging over the bench, looking up and imagining pictures in the clouds.

"You... You know I love this time of day," Jamie blurted, chilled and smiling whilst letting smoke escape from his mouth. He was a slim, lanky boy; neck-length blonde hair brushed off to the side under his hat.

"Ah, same," agreed Harvey, flinging the stub of his joint behind a leafless tree beside them. Now, two years ago, Harvey could've been described as the same as Jamie but with short, brown hair and green eyes instead of blonde hair and blue eyes. However, he bulked up after having enough of being bullied. He wasn't known around school and the neighbourhood for bulking up; in addition to gaining muscle, he was mostly known around the estate as the guy who burnt out cigarette stubs in his victim's eyes.

As for Jamie, he was the thief of the trio; although coming across as an idiot at times, he was the brains behind the jobs they did and the arrangements for the purchase of drugs. He did time in jail, about three years before being released back onto the streets, getting caught attempting to rob the corner shop on Readmarsh Road on his own.

Tony rolled his eyes, being the one sitting in the middle of his sidemen.

"Why do you always have to agree with everything I say?" asked Jamie, tension stupidly rising for no reason.

"Will you two just shut the fuck up," Tony ordered. His wish was their command, shutting up and snarling at each other behind his back. "Now, are youse bringing lasses to me sesh in a couple weeks?" Even asking the question, he knew the answer of both men.

"Nar, na," they said together, going red, trying their best not to look at Lesterson.

"Thought not," he sniggered.

"*Thought not*," Jamie echoed – with a grunt – at a volume where he hoped Tony wouldn't have heard.

"You wha'?" Tony snapped, glaring at the boy to his left.

"Nothing." Jamie winced.

They sat there in silence, taking in their fellow druggies slumping in the corners of the park, in a world of their own. Harvey sighed and was eager to make more conversation, with the weed wearing off too quickly, hiding his and the other's bags without them noticing as a policeman and policewoman passed with suspicion, keeping an eye out for the scum of the town.

"So... happening with this lass then you *constantly* go on about?" Harvey finally asked.

Tony glanced at Harvey, wondering what stage he was at with Isabella. He didn't want to come across as being too forward, but not taking things as slow just so he could possibly show her up in front of his pals.

"Good. Good. She's totally interested," his response was.

"And are you interested?" Harvey asked, hesitantly.

"I'm only interested in one thing." Tony coughed, winking, and pointing his nose down.

It had taken a minute but the cronies had finally caught on to what he meant. They both laughed, whooping and patting Tony on the back.

"So... when?"

"At me session that am havin' in a couple weeks."

"Where is it at?" said Jamie, including himself in the conversation.

"Mine. Obviously," replied Tony, wondering why Jamie would even ask that question. Both Tony and Harvey – and even Jamie, to an extent – knew that if a party was hosted at either of the cronies' homes then nobody would show. Tony's was the place to be, and everyone knew it. "And let's just say that by the end of it..." Tony arrogantly gestured at his manhood, "Isabella's gonna be riding on this fella." They all laughed, especially with Jamie standing out from the group, snorting with every chuckle.

"It's goin' to be a belta," Harvey said excitedly, rising and leading the group along the crumbled pathway deep into an army of trees.

"Yeah. But it's going to be either my way, or no way. That's the way it is, and that's the way it'll always be."

And the ones who knew Tony personally didn't take that lightly, he meant what he said.

4

All Anthony could hear bellowing from his daughter's bedroom from above him, where he sat at the dining table in the kitchen, was the cackle of three teenage witches, brewing up a potion for the night; a potion filled with sugar, films, and even more cackling.

Up in the room, Hannah and Jess laid across the bed haphazardly whilst the host of the slumber night sat on the chair that matched her desk in the far corner of her room, enraptured by the tinging of her phone when a new message from Tony appeared, unaware of the conversation that her friends were having.

"I only got with him for free food," Jess admitted, bursting out into heaps of laughter with Hannah.

"Oh, shut up, Jess. You'll do anything for free food," Hannah joked, noticing that Bella wasn't laughing along.

"Yeah, but at least I got something out of it. It's not my fault Billy Curtsey snogged ya under the bleachers at school and never spoke to you again," Jess fired back.

Hannah acted like it meant nothing to her, but she knew that she didn't have a better comeback. She glanced at Isabella who was still fixed on her phone, and thought to take a shot at her.

"What's wrong, Bella? You just embarrassed because you're scared to admit that you kissed him in year five in the playground?" Hannah said, sniggering.

"In fact, I'm not scared," Isabella clarified. "I'm getting more than you two put together because Tony is messaging me now," she mocked. Isabella's besties whooped proudly; not for Isabella getting a steady boyfriend, but for her finally revealing his name and that there is something going on. "He's actually saying he's going to *work* at the moment, so he can't speak much," she said haughtily, her nose pointed in the air. Muttering to one another, and with Isabella muttering to herself as if Tony was really in her hands – not paying attention to the girls on the bed – Jess and Hannah seemed sceptical of who this Tony guy really was and what he was all about.

"So… what's this Tony like, then?" Jess questioned.

"Well," Bella started to answer, finally moving away from the vibrating phone, and turning to the girls, and followed up, "at first, he seemed a bit rough around the edges, but once I got to know him, he is the nicest guy I've met." She took one last glance at the final message Tony had sent before he started his evening shift. "Oh."

The words on the rectangular screen shook her. "He's just said that he would like to invite me and anyone I want to something he calls a *sesh*..." They all shrugged at each other. "Think it's like a party," she answered their unasked – but thought – query. She continued on, "in two weeks at his house."

They all screamed, overjoyed that they've been informally invited to their first ever house party, oblivious of the risk of the inclusion of alcoholic beverages.

"OMG! OMG! OMG! OMG!" Jess shouted, elated, fanning away the arriving tears of joy.

Hannah calmed her down, directing Jess' hysterical breathing pattern into a more rhythmic form.

"Tell us the deets... before Jess has a heart attack," pleaded Hannah.

"They must need snacks. Do they have snacks? I'll definitely bring snacks," Jess added, in a frenzy, bouncing frantically on the edge of Isabella's bed. "They must need snacks. Do they have snacks? I'll bring snacks," she repeated, unable to let Isabella have her say.

"Jess, you need to cool it," Hannah informed her, patting Jess' shoulder.

"Yeah, I mean, it's not for another two weeks," reminded Bella. "Besides, I want to see how this date goes first," she quietly revealed.

"I can bring Flakes, Toffee Crisps, Lindor's – Lindor's are my favourites – and others like Twirl and..." She stopped, stunned, silent.

"You wha'?" Hannah tilted her head with a simper. "Sugar. Honey. Iced. Tea!"

They leaped off the bed and straight into Isabella's arms, congratulating her like she had accepted a proposal. They all beamed with glee but talked over one another, having trouble communicating and knowing when to let one of them finally let a clear sentence out.

"Yeah, I know! It's great, isn't it? He's taking me to Cheryl's Italian on Cherry Lane."

Hannah *awe*'d. Jess held back the tears.

"That's so cute. Because that's where your dad proposed to your mother," Jess said, tenderly stroking Isabella's arm. They all made their way back to the bed, Isabella sitting in the middle and the other two on either side of her. "Yes, we can help you find something amazing to wear," she continued, the idea just springing to mind. "When is it?"

"Tomorrow night," Isabella announced regretfully, actually liking the idea of her two best friends helping her get ready for her big first ever date; also mindful of the reality that she *didn't* have anything to wear.

The girls on both sides of Isabella forced her to rise.

"... And that's why God invented shopping," they both said gleefully, eager to get Isabella into town for fittings of the finest dresses – forget about boys, or men, this was the absolute dream for all three of them.

5

With Tony as confident as ever in a white polo, slim-fit jeans, and his hair combed for once, waiting at the entrance to the best restaurant in Castlehead, Isabella sat in the back of her dad's car, holding back the nerves and sweat so her father wouldn't notice in the mirror above him; he didn't know she was going on a date, she just told him she was meeting with the girls for a couple of hours out for food.

But deep down, too, Isabella started to doubt how long she could keep up this charade.

It was a tight squeeze, but Isabella narrowly managed to make her way out of the car; the door hitting the curb so Isabella had to breathe in until bones were noticeable to get through. Her hair was wild, curled, but flowed down her shoulders like a wavy river. Her eyes were expressively large, showing a ray of emotions including nerves and true happiness – an emotion that she hadn't experienced in a long time.

Happiness, Isabella thought as she walked down the cobblestone aisle toward the red carpet and the gleaming lights shining through the windows, *is an emotion which anyone is capable of feeling at any moment. Yet, true happiness comes when you know something feels right and you live in the moment, not thinking about the past or future.*

With each step, Bella felt more comfortable moving toward Tony – who was in a world of his own until he got a glimpse of that astounding looking girl on the verge of womanhood – as she stepped further away from her dad who was thinking of driving away even before she was out of sight. His heart resisted it, looking back at the knee-length black dress with faint green roots sprouting up to from luminescent red roses on her shoulders and around her waist. Her impulsive strut down into the location of Anthony and Sharron's first date had brought back memories he was unwillingly remembering; memories he hoped that would have cast away by now, by now knowing what the future held for the couple.

6: THEN

A young Anthony, still growing into his body, wearing a suit which was one size too big for him, opened the back door closest to the curb of the cab to let out a radiant, classy, young lady by the name of Sharron Rose.

He stood, transfixed. His eyes the only function of his body moving, tracking the woman he had once thought would never go for a man like him. Her blanche dress was covered with pink, scattered roses just starting to bloom as if it was the pure season of summer. She sparkled luminously like a delicate glaze as she strutted down what she acted out to be a catwalk so all the men their age could snap their heads in her direction away from their own dates.

Wow, what a woman, her date thought, proudly following her, envisioning how lucky he'll be if this date went well and according to plan.

Although a woman in Anthony's eyes, Sharron was only a girl of eighteen and nowhere near the pinnacle of the pure beauty that would come with her twenties. And although described to her overprotective, upper-class parents as a confident, charming bloke capable of already supporting himself at nineteen, Anthony Eccleby announced bravely at the beginning of the date that he grew up in what was – and still is – known as the *dodgy end* of Castlehead. Sometimes double, even triple shifts barely supported the Eccleby family, forcing Anthony to start full-time work at fifteen and leave school early; managing to scrape in just enough to keep the family going in the cheap-rented apartment they survived in for the majority of his life.

Knowing from the first time Sharron was briefly mentioned that Anthony was more than *into* this Sharron Rose, Anthony's parents scraped together their monthly payments and gave him half of the total pay. And with the kind gesture, Anthony finally built up the courage to ask her out.

To his astonishment, she said, "Yes".

But Sharron knew too well that if she spoke the truth about Anthony's background, her parents wouldn't give her consent, as they envisioned their princess saddling on the back of a white horse controlled by a knight in shining armour – or something along those lines. In reality, her parents expected Sharron to at least get with someone in their class.

"So," Anthony began, trying his best to relax and comprehend that he was sitting opposite the most extravagant woman he had seen; in addition, sitting opposite the most extravagant woman he had seen in the poshest restaurant in town. "Tell me about yourself."

"Well, I've lived here all my life," she started to respond as Anthony thought, *Good start. Starting off with a general question.* "You see, I'm down on Eccose Road."

A splash of the complimentary water given to the couple when they had been seated came spitting out of his mouth, choking in disbelief.

"Christ!" he coughed, slowly maintaining a regular breathing pattern. "Must be nice." He tried the sip of water again, successfully swallowing the refreshing fluid.

"It's not too bad, but it can get very stuck up." She wasn't wrong. Being the most wealthy street in all of Castlehead, all the neighbours – including her parents

– believed that classy children born and raised on this street shouldn't be seen playing, but devoting their life to high educational literature, and aiming for the most well-paid jobs in Castlehead, some even the most well-paid in all of England. This was mainly due to Castlehead's RGS being in the top fifteen percent of England's exceeding exam rate.

"Ah, right." He tapped his fingers on the table to the rhythm of the live piano that was being played. "Still living with parents?" he asked.

"Yeah," she sighed, seeming to be disappointed in herself. "I haven't quite reached that level of what is expected from an eighteen-year-old raised on Eccose Road," she groaned.

"To me, you have."

She hid her face, blushing with a cheeky smile.

They talked through the evening and into the night; the type of talk you have when you're just in the moment, forgetting the troubles oneself may have and what is going on in their lives; losing track of time.

"You didn't like your food?" asked Sharron, searching for other customers in the deserted restaurant.

"No..." Anthony realised that – although his roast lamb dinner was stunning – only half a plate had been consumed. "It was lovely," he said.

They both laughed, and Anthony signalled for the waiter to bring them the bill.

7: NOW

They talked through the evening and into the night; you know, the kind of conversation where nothing else matters and you just enjoy the company. Well, for

Isabella, anyways. In his mind, Tony just wanted to know how fast this was going to escalate into something a little more passionate.

"You didn't like your food?" asked Isabella, searching for other customers in the isolated restaurant.

Tony glanced down at his full plate of food.

"Erm... no." He flicked through for the correct reply in his not-so educated mind so he wouldn't blow it. "Guess I just got lost in your eyes." Although his toes curled, it was effective as his date signalled over the waiter who had been serving them for the entire duration of their date, trying to hide her clear blushing. Her face was as red as a rose.

The waiter didn't want to be there; the employee who only did it for the minimum wage so they could just piss it up on nights out in the town and useless accessories for video games. He shuffled through the tables and chairs all tucked in, tripping over the ends of the table cloths that covered the tables, and stepping into wet marshes of food from babies and young children who complained that the food that they received wasn't what they had wanted. The lean, adolescent worker finally arrived with a choice of paying by cash in one hand and paying by card in the other, in a world of his own with a facial expression so bland that it would make a cantankerous, depressed, old man seem like the happiest guy on Earth.

Isabella and Tony exchanged looks of offering to pay, leading into exchanges of vocal discussion on who was willing to pay. They both were for that matter, but came to the conclusion that the bill would be split 50/50.

"Thank you," the waiter said in an unconvincing cheerful manner, tearing the receipt from the wireless card machine which Isabella had used with her contactless card to make the transaction; Tony agreed to pay her his share as soon as possible. Waiting for a tip, the boy of a similar age to Isabella gestured for a little extra in which Isabella went through with, explaining to him that the food was delicious in every way possible, his service lacked confidence and welcoming comfort.

Tony allowed Isabella to lead the way out of the restaurant and into the chilly Sunday night. They stood on the curb, shivering, waiting for their ride to arrive, and uncomfortably smiling at each other every fifteen seconds until one of them said a word.

"I really enjoyed tonight," Isabella said, genuinely telling the truth, not stretching it, slowly manoeuvring her hand into the grasp of Tony's. His was rough, but gentle, whilst hers was smooth and pure.

Tony didn't reply, but gave a hint of happiness as he couldn't resist the gentle touch of her skin on his. With one hand still in Bella's grasp, Tony's other reached down into his pocket for a small carton that showed the inside of what lungs eventually look like when someone can get addicted to smoking.

Isabella leaped back instantly, backing away from the sight of that small cylinder of porous paper containing a rod of chopped up tobacco leaf that Tony popped in between his dry lips. Also reaching for a lighter, Tony looked at Isabella curiously, as if he didn't know what he was doing wrong.

"What?" he mumbled, glancing down at the cigarette. "You don't like them?" He snatched it from his lips and teased Isabella with it, chasing her like what children would do in the playground if one of them pretended to have a germ and chased the other kids around until they tagged one of them. She was split between begging him to stop and bursting into joyous laughter.

"No, I don't like it," she finally responded, trapped between the wall of the closed restaurant and Tony, slowly creeping up towards her with the cigarette in hand.

"Have you ever tried it?" he said, slithering up even more towards her until their noses touched.

"No."

"Well, how do you know you don't like it if you've never tried it?"

Isabella, embarrassed, replied, "Because my mother told me it wasn't good."

The mood had shifted back to uncomfortable and serious, with Isabella surprised that Tony didn't laugh, but handed her a clean one out of the packet and nodded as if to tell her to give it a go. She was reluctant and attempted to hand the cigarette back to its owner. But, Tony being Tony, he declined it as he was acting to be busy, lighting his own cigarette.

"It's not gonna kill ya," he said after the first puff of smoke left his mouth.

That must be why his finger nails are that yellow, she thought, quizzing. *But what's the worst that could happen?*

She sighed with a little "Okay."

Giving into the pressure and temptation, Isabella finally accepted the offer. Holding it in between her middle and index fingers, she examined it, having no idea what to do; the thought of her parent's reaction if he'd ever find out about this raced through her mind. She tried to shake it out as Tony handed her the lighter. One flick of the light, no flame. Two flicks of the light, no flame. Three flicks, then a bright yellow and orange flame appeared. She gazed into it before any further progression into the feeling of what it is like to smoke.

"Bella?" Tony clicked his fingers. "You okay?"

"Wha'? Yeah," she said in a daze. Forgetting what she had just seen, Isabella continued on to put the cigarette in her mouth – it tasted rotten – and lit it. What she didn't know, though, was that you shouldn't inhale first if you are not used to it. She hacked up the smoke, but got the hang of it quite quickly, and as she exhaled frequent puffs of smoke, puffs of the thought of her parents and what they thought exhaled out, too.

8

It was late, but not too late. Knowing it was a school night, Isabella rejected the offer to head back to Tony's, yet she was very tempted. Being the first one to be dropped off in the taxi, she got a farewell peck on the cheek by Tony through the cab window.

She turned and headed for the doors of her house, gliding down the pathway, imagining what the future would hold for them both; perhaps a white summer wedding on a beach where she would wait on shore at the altar next to her bridesmaids, Hannah and Jess, with all her family in the front rows of chairs awaiting the groom's arrival on a snow white stallion, wearing a smooth suit with a rose clipped on one side. Or even a marriage kept in secret because their parents wouldn't give their blessings as their backgrounds and place in society wouldn't like it, a wedding in the ruins of a church just outside woodlands where no one would find them until a time when they have long passed on and one of their descendants would accidentally stumble upon them on a hiking trip with their family, and so tests would be done on her and Tony's lifeless bodies, cleaned, and finally put to peace – buried in the local cemetery...

... Together forever.

The faint yell of her name snapped her out of whatever she had dreamed of, and a knock followed as Anthony tried to get her to open the doors on her own accord.

"Bella, just open the door," he ordered once more. She quickly shook her head and proceeded to twist the doorknob and enter the house to immediately be struck with the question, "Are you okay?"

"Yeah, fine." Her response was plain and unpersuasive. She acted as if nothing had happened and went on just to say that she and her friends had a good night, and that they were planning on doing it again a week from the upcoming Saturday; all while her father glared at her with his arms folded and his expression stern, emotionless. He was thinking. He was worried.

But all he could respond with was a plain old "Okay," wishing he could actually get through to his daughter by actually communicating, instead of having one-line conversations or arguments which jeopardised their relationship which had hung by a thread for many years.

With a skip in her step and a bewitching grin, Isabella started to ascend the stairs to her bedroom to get ready for bed.

"Bella, wait there," Anthony ordered. With his nose scrunched up like a pig's, he asked, "Do you smell smoke?"

His daughter's nerves shook with her frozen body. The thoughts of the consequences that would come with Anthony catching her red-handed started to race through her mind again.

"No," she answered, with a squeak in her voice and terror on her face. Along with the trouble of trying to avoid eye contact with her father, Isabella spun back around and raced up to her room. "Stop asking me questions!" She slammed her door, and Anthony didn't hear from his daughter for the rest of the night.

Slumping, Anthony dragged his feet along the floor into the kitchen, collapsing onto the head chair at the top of the dining table. His head was down and cupped in his hands, shaking back and forth.

"I can't get through to her," he said under his breath.

I know I said that she was growing up and that she needed space, but you need to talk to her before something happens. You know, I know, and I think, deep down, she knows she's not exactly herself.

9: THEN

Anthony offered to hold the door open for his date as they left.

The sky was clear, hundreds of stars were visible as they accompanied the shining moon as the night came to a close. Mesmerised, Anthony had to pinch himself to make sure that the night he'd just had wasn't a dream. Watching the beauty that was Sharron Rose; her dress and hair flowed in the midnight breeze as they strolled through the empty streets of the town, Anthony was still mesmerised by Sharron – a woman he believed had been crafted by the angels out of the stars.

They continued to chat as the night came to a close, both of them wishing the night was everlasting. Not getting the bus or a taxi, they decided to walk home, hoping the night could last a few minutes longer. It was Anthony who dropped his date off first.

Sharron's home on Eccose Road was new, fresh, clean. It stood out from the rest of the street as it had been completed that same year, in addition to it being the first house of its kind to have been given a name – except Michael Manor.

This is home, Sharron thought as she glanced back and forth from the stunning boy, Anthony to her home. It wasn't until her parents had waved at her from the glowing, white front door, unamused, that the thought drifted away never to be thought of again. Sharron's parents glared at Anthony, taking no notice of their disappointed daughter who made her way down the wide, stone drive, trying to ignore her parents. Anthony felt discomfort when he had realised that Sharron's mother and father didn't take their eyes off him, eyebrows pointed down and arms folded in unison. He knew he wasn't wanted and so, without Sharron noticing, walked without a fuss to the end of the wealthiest street in Castlehead and back onto the main road.

"You lied to us," Sharron's mother said with Anthony out of view and her husband shaking his head, his stomach turning in disgust whenever he met eye contact with his daughter. All Sharron could do was just hang her head in shame as her parents led her back into the house.

However, stopping in the doorway of the house, Sharron grabbed the handle behind her to close the door, but afraid to see that Anthony wasn't in sight; afraid that this was just a one-time thing, afraid that her parents had been right all along.

All that 'stepping out of society's bubble' talk by her best friend sounded ridiculous to her now, feeling like an idiot for actually not caring what her parents and so-called friends said and accepting to go out with someone who was in the minor leagues compared to her.

What would they say on Monday at school? She thought, weeping herself to sleep after a screaming fest with her parents.

The date went so well, but did I just blow it? Anthony thought as he rode on the lonely bus home.

Chapter Four

The Winds of Change

1: NOW

The Winds of Change, by Sara Kelly, was a novel that Isabella had found on the last night in Wardle Gardens in one of her mother's chest of drawers. It hadn't been known to anyone that she had found it and kept it for herself as a way to remember her mother. She read one page a day since her twelfth birthday, resulting in her to be on the last page when she came home from school the day after her date with Tony.

The writing was small, but the book was big. Being over one thousand pages, *The Winds of Change* explored how people can change when they are influenced by their social group, or when they're mad, scared, or stressed. Like her mother, each sentence drew Isabella in with the author's unique writing style and storytelling. It had her gripping on to the edge of the bed with every sentence, at times, wanting to read another.

2

However, *The Winds of Change* wouldn't be her focus until later that night – yet, the winds of change could only happen gradually – whereas walking into school on that dull Monday morning, her focus was on telling Hannah and Jess how great Tony was. It was as if she was gliding through the halls of the school, still dressed appropriately for school, but with the smell of smoke on her breath, causing all who would usually love to be her friend to retreat.

She roamed up and down through the narrow aisles which the wooden chairs and desks neatly formed, trying to find her seat. This was her second lesson of the day and, as she slouched back into her designated seat haphazardly, the teacher-in-training called out the register.

"Err..." She ran her finger down the list of students. "Right, first, do we have Emily Kent?"

A petite girl with glasses on and a blue tint in her eyes raised her hand and yelled "Here" to signify that she was present in class and ready to learn.

"Gerald Stolk... Henry Carmen... " With every name called, a repetitive raise of the hand or a yell came after. The list went on, and on, and on until the teacher got all the way down the list to Isabella's name. "Isabella Rose-Eccleby."

All that came with Isabella's immediate response was a grunt.

"Isabella, please respond properly, and have some respect for Miss Tiddman," the class' usual teacher said, surprised, writing notes and points on how the teacher-in-training was doing.

"Fine," Isabella sneered, flaring her nostrils at the new assigned teacher. "*Here...*"

Miss Tiddman put a tick next to Isabella's name, just like how she marked all the other's before her.

"Can someone be ever so kind to take this sheet to the attendance office?" said Miss Tiddman, clearing her throat as she rose from her desk chair. And without hesitation, Isabella lazily raised her hand, proudly accepting the job. "Ah, thank you..." She skimmed down the register once again. "... Isabella."

Bella shoved her chair into the desk behind her dangerously as she rose, walked over to the teacher, and plucked the A4 sheet from Tiddman's tiny hands, jerking her arm.

The halls were empty as the lessons were on, and she did as she was told – but not for the purpose of showing Tiddman that she was a teacher's pet. It took a minute, but Isabella made it to the attendance office. Located near the reception, Isabella had to walk through all the subject blocks and through the canteen to make it up to where the reception was. There was a line of three glass doors; the middle being double doors which led to the main reception and the exit, the left door took her into the Head's office, and the right was the door that she was looking for, the door that would take her into the attendance office.

She lightly knocked twice on the door, waiting for the staff member to wave at her to enter. Isabella slightly opened the door just enough for her hand and register paper to slip through. The staff member took it gently from Isabella's rough fingers, thanking her as she left. Isabella sighed, leaning against the now closed door behind her, she started to walk back down the hall, passing a student wearing a full Nike tracksuit with messy, black hair within the clutches of Mr Hope, a tall, intimidating teacher who never let out a smile. Her eyes followed the teacher dragging the student by the collar up to the Head's office, and as that door closed behind them, Isabella heard what could only be described as World War Three, but only with talks of exclusion and calling the police.

A shiver ran down Isabella's spine, suddenly. A chill. A vision. Isabella looked around, and there she was, still at the school. Although, the overcast clouds were now grim and black. Thunder shook the school once... or twice. She couldn't tell. If the school didn't seem empty to Isabella before, it sure did now. The lights went out, and darkness spread across the building. Defining screams precipitated through the narrow halls, and rattled Bella's ears, causing her to scream herself. She was screaming, she knew she was, but it didn't feel like it. The screams, not from students, drained all the screams that Isabella could muster, crumbling to the floor into a little ball, allowing the walls and the roof to close in.

She was trapped. She was alone. She was isolated.

"Bella? Wake up! Wake up!"

She uncontrollably rolled back and forth in her ball, feeling like someone was forcing her to do it. Isabella's eyes were shut tight, weeping mercifully, begging for whatever was happening to stop in between little screams and whimpers.

"Wake up!" another voice said, yet this one sounded familiar, unlike the last one. "Wake up," the voice repeated.

Did she really have a choice? Not really. But she knew she didn't want to.

"Do I have to?" she asked the voices, sniffing.

"Well, yeah. You're on the floor, curled up in a ball in the middle of the main hall where everyone can see you." This voice was familiar, all too familiar. "Come on, get up." A pair of hands that felt like handcuffs wrapped around her wrists, and a pair that feel like a puppy's clawless paws? It was Hannah and Jess. "What in the h-e-l-l were you doing on the floor?" the voice of Hannah asked, lifting Isabella up by one arm and Jess by the other.

Isabella finally opened her eyes to reveal, not grim, black clouds, but a yellow sun glaring through the windows and blue skies.

"D-Did you feel that, too?" Isabella winced. The pair shrugged, hiding the worry that overcame them when they saw their best friend in that state from a little bit of thunder and a couple of children jokily screaming.

"There was a bit of thunder, but that's it. Are you sure you're okay?"

Bella looked around, puffing and panting, desperate to catch her breath. She broke from her friends' grasp and slid back, almost losing her balance just after getting it back.

"Y-Ye-Yeah. I'm fine." She turned, then directly launched herself toward the nearest exit. Hannah and Jess tried to stop her from leaving school without permission, but couldn't catch up to the speed which Isabella was running at. Even the receptionist couldn't stop her.

The front gates were only open for the sole purpose of students leaving with permission from a parent, guardian, or teacher if they're weren't feeling well, or if they had a scheduled appointment – not for escaping. Even without her friends chasing her, Isabella ran as fast as she could, like if she was running to win a race at the Olympics, or running away from a demon that lurked behind her, eyes as yellow as a cat's and chunks of it's hair ripped out, constantly smiling, but not a happy smile, with an urge to get his pale hands on her.

3: THEN

A seven-year-old Isabella was trapped, alone, and isolated, hiding under the climbing frame in the playground from the big kids who pushed and shoved their way through queues of the smaller, defenceless children such as Isabella.

She whimpered like a puppy being left alone in the rain to fend for itself, no one taking notice – not even the teachers. Her back against a blue metal post, keeping the slide stable, she slid down in sadness and despair, wrapping her arms around her knees. Upright, she curled up in the shadows of the structure, wary of the kids that ran past, cheering like any normal kid should at break time.

Isabella brushed her hair away from her face. In a pool of her own tears by the time break had ended, Isabella would have rather stayed to soak and melt away in the water than get up to finally reveal herself to the harsh sun and head back to her classroom.

She ignored the whistle that had been blown by her teacher, Ms Hart, and carried on crying, until a knock on the slide caught her attention.

"Are you okay?" an innocent, lively voice asked.

Isabella, although nodding weakly, still tried to hide her face within the enclosed space of her arms wrapping around her head as she continued to look down.

"Come on, Jess," another girl, named Hannah, said as she ran over. "What's the matter?" The other girl, who Isabella had just learnt her name was Jess, gestured toward Bella herself. "Oh," Hannah added, with no further comment.

"Come on, it's okay." Jess tried to persuade Isabella to come out from under the shadows and into the light. "Please." There was no verbal response from Bella, who was not sniffling. Jess huffed and jerked her head down towards the girl who she wanted to help, descending down to a level which suited Jess so she could gently place her smooth, delicate hand on Isabella's forearm and lead her out into the sunlight, where she would properly introduce herself and Hannah.

"I'm Isabella," said Isabella, wiping away the last of her tears, innocently chuckling. It progressed into a full-on hysterical laugh, with her new friends, Hannah, and Jess, joining in; the both of them completely lost to why they were laughing along.

But if it made Isabella happy, it made them happy.

If her father had told Isabella in the morning that by the end of the day she would become lifelong friends with two of the most gentle, kind, sometimes brutally honest people in Castlehead, then she would've called him crazy, amused at the complex theory.

The newly formed trio wrapped their arms around one another's shoulders, and hopped and skipped their way to their class.

4: NOW

The stitches in her lower abdomen started to take a toll on Isabella's stamina as she had been sprinting for at least ten whole minutes now, and with no sense of direction – in her current state of mind, because of what had just taken place in front of the whole school – and no final destination, she ran as far as her body could take her.

Yes, she ran and ran with no destination *in mind*, however she knew too well where her body was taking her. And before she knew it, the teenager stood in the middle of a remote neighbourhood; a neighbourhood that seemed to be out of place within Castlehead.

But once she heard the soothing voice of Tony Lesterson bellowing out her name at the end of the road, Isabella exhaled, relaxed, indicating her relief.

Finally comprehending that she was in no nightmare now, it was a promising reality. And with Tony proving that he is dedicated and willing to take time out of his day to check on the girl he had been only seeing for a couple of weeks, Isabella knew she was in good hands, and there could be no wrong.

Running even faster than she was whilst trying to escape that demonic hellhole that was her sixth form, Tony wasn't prepared for Isabella dashing towards him, cheering his name, letting the street know his name, leaping into his arms and finally being able to relieve the curse within her by giving him a much deserved kiss.

5

Tony led Isabella to what he called home, supporting her with his broad shoulder as they both managed to squeeze through the doorway into the, possibly, diseased house.

The house looked like it had been hit by a bomb; clothes on the floor, carpets torn, cold as a freezer, and smelled of alcohol and drugs. If this was any other day, Isabella would have been disgusted, but at this point in time, she didn't care where she was, only who she was with.

They shuffled to the left into the lounge, releasing from their links.

"Take a seat... if you can," instructed Tony, turning back into the hall and into the half-functioning kitchen. Isabella froze, examining the room, noticing the large figure collapsed on the couch in front of her, barely awake.

"H... Hi." Bella gulped, timidly tapping his freakishly skinny shoulder, capable of seeing the bone clearly.

There was no response, only a weak grunt. And it had occurred to Isabella – when she saw the beer bottle slipping out of his numb hand – that he had passed out.

"This is typical of him." Tony said from behind her. She jumped in freight.

"Sorry?" she squeaked.

"This is my dad." Tony had a glass of what was meant to be water in each hand. "This is what he's basically been like since Mother... well..." Tony looked down to the floor, attempting to hide his face which turned a light pink. He coughed away his choked-up voice and continued. "Come on. Let him rest." He gestured with his head for Isabella to follow him up the stairs to his bedroom.

With every subtle step, the staircase creaked, with Tony trying not to spill drops of water and Isabella following, her spine tingling as she tiptoed closer and closer to the bedroom. She was halted by Tony's large body, blocking the entry. Her gulps were louder now, desperately trying to avoid eye contact.

"Sorry about the mess," he said, noticing her head snapping from left to right rapidly. "You okay?"

"Hm?" She finally glanced up as if she was just standing there, waiting to be allowed entry. "Yeah, fine."

Tony nodded, pleased. He turned, carefully placing the glasses on the sturdy floorboards – carpets hadn't been placed past the stairs – and opened the door which swung open, almost detaching from its hinges.

Politely, Isabella picked up the glasses without being asked. Seeing Tony go to the far end of the room and sit down on his mattress – and that's all his bed was, a mattress – looking out of the window, Isabella felt somewhat more comfortable than she did when she first entered the house. He sighed. It was a sigh of distress, a sigh of anger, a sigh of sadness. And from this sigh, Isabella knew that something was wrong.

She glared around the room for a place to put the drinks, but that wasn't all she was looking around the room for. The room gave her shivers, not the shiver that she regularly felt more recently, but a shiver – a tremble – from the cold. Bella didn't want to intrude, or act as if she was being nosy, and decided to skim the room whilst placing the glasses firmly on the ground next to her; cramped, unsanitary.

Lonely, she thought. *How can anyone live in conditions like this*?

There was nothing in the room apart from the two beings, a mattress, a small pile of clothes that looked like they hadn't been washed in weeks, and a lamp. She had noticed that the lamp was switched on, she also noticed that the sun was glaring through the blinds attached to the window.

She stood as still as a scarecrow, rubbing her arm, trying to think how or what she could do to help. She inched closer to where Tony had sat and not said a word. His head was in his hands now, his eyes following the little beetles that scattered themselves around the house.

"It wasn't always like this, you know," he finally said out of nowhere. "And *HIM* downstairs wasn't the alcoholic druggie that he is now, not even moving to go for a piss."

"What happened?" she asked, her shadow looming over him, with the thought that the question was a bit of a stretch.

"My mother, that's what happened."

Isabella crouched down beside him, accepting a cigarette that he had kindly offered, ready to hear what happened.

6: THEN

It was a time that any child shouldn't remember because of how long ago it was when Tony's mother left. Not *left* as in that she divorced his father. In fact, Karen helped Tony's father to quit drinking and drugs. She got his life back on track, and after three months, they were married.

It was Karen that had the job, not her husband, although he had been looking. He was more the stay-at-home husband, soon to be the stay-at-home father, than anything else. He would have the house spotless, sparkling, so clean that you could see your reflection in the kitchen benches. But what Karen had wasn't the best paid job in the world. Being a customer assistant at the Tesco that Tony would eventually end up working at, it was either take it or leave it. At only £4 an hour, full-time too, Karen did offer to go over her contracted hours to gain more; double, sometimes even triple shifts. And somehow, she would still make time for her husband, but with the unplanned baby due at a time when business was bad, and the store issued cutbacks, it wasn't the best time for the Lestersons.

Lucky enough, she hadn't been fired, however, she had lost her full-time role. The manager had said, as persuasively as he could, that he knew the baby would be arriving anytime and so thought working only a couple of days a week would help. Besides, they did want this baby to be healthy... although it was said to be a mistake, accidental, unexpected. Impossible.

The father of the child didn't know how it could've happened either.

And before they knew it, little Tony Lesterson was born. Karen loved the rascal to death, working her butt off to give him the best life. However, how can you give a child much without money?

Exactly.

Being away from work for a good number of months caused Karen and her husband to get into trouble with the police and child services. But she wouldn't give up, telling them where they could stick it when they tried to take her precious son away.

Her husband on the other hand, doing what he did best, attempted stealing from numerous supermarkets and retail outlets around the area, ending up getting himself arrested for attempted robbery. Eight months he was in the town prison for, rotting in his cell that was no bigger than an average sized bedroom. Welts and bruises emerged on his face and around his body when he was released from the several beatings he got from his fellow inmates who ended up sharing the cell with him, all because he thought he could pick a fight with people who slit people's throats to get arrested.

For those eight months, the remaining Lesterson family lived on rations of food and a limited supply of water; even with the help of the Tesco store manager, Johnathan, Karen started having thoughts that her baby Tony wouldn't even make it to the age on one if they kept living the way they did.

He did eventually get out, yet not as soon as he – or his family – hoped. Because of these altercations with the fellow inmates, and hitting a number of officers in the process of the fights being broken up, Karen's husband had to do more time. An extra six months.

It was around this time when Karen started to have second thoughts about her husband, and if she had really changed him.

The six months had passed and it was time for his release; making sure that it really was, he didn't assault anyone or did anything stupid enough to keep him locked away from the outside world and risking never seeing the sun again.

Prison had once again changed Karen's husband. He was a different guy, and Karen didn't know where the person she had married went. It appeared that he went back to his old, savage ways, that included drugs, alcohol, smoking, and steadily converting back to stealing – this time, not getting caught. These habits, or *hobbies* (is what he called them) made him a threat, letting the drink and drugs get to him and make the atmosphere of their home uneasy. This disgraceful behaviour lasted for years, ending up with him becoming sick, physically, and mentally. So sick that he wouldn't even remember when awakening that the night before, he had maliciously assaulted both his wife and Tony.

These conditions that would eventually become the norm in the Lesterson household drove Karen to the brink of her breaking point, and caused her to finally reveal the truth.

7

The truth had been revealed on a day when the sky was clear and the sun shone brightly directly above the house. Although being midday, there was no sight of Karen's partner since the night before, having one of his typical – now, daily – rants before storming off to a different bar every time, so Karen and Tony wouldn't know where he would be so they wouldn't find him. And despite the devotion she once had for him had drifted off long ago, Karen didn't want him to wind up stabbed to death in a deserted alleyway where no one would find him.

It took him a number of tries, but he finally succeeded in getting the door unlocked, stumbling into the hall. He swayed back and forth, bouncing off the walls like a ping-pong ball. He flung his leather jacket on the floor, kicked his boots off causing dents in the wall to appear almost instantly.

The sound of the boots crashing into the walls sounded like thunder, with Karen adding to the escalating crashes as she stomped down the stairs, unafraid of her husband and knowing that if she stomped any harder the stairs would end up collapsing under her.

"For Christ's sake! Are you for fucking real?" Karen had never spoken like this towards her partner before, previously fearing the punishment that she would have to endure, showing no remorse this time round.

"G... G... Get off me back," he spat, stumbling on his words along with stumbling over the obstacle course that was his boots and coat right in front of Karen. He fell face first, expecting help. She normally did... when she was his wife.

"I should just let you lie there and rot like the disgrace you are," she hissed, letting out all the anger she was able to contain.

"Has he fallen again?" an eleven-year-old Tony yelled from the top of the stairs, taking each step cautiously.

He was timid and weak, his hair a mop upon his head that hid his eyes. Wearing a vest revealed his twig arms, shorts showing his pigeon legs, and unable to hide the fact that you could see his facial structure from a mile off.

"Tony, get behind me. Now!" his mother ordered, using her arm to restrain him from getting any closer to the man struggling to maintain a steady balance.

"Tony," the drunk said, relieved, following up with a grin as ugly as a pirate's; teeth black. "Come to Papa."

"He's going nowhere," Karen warned, answering for her son.

"He's my son, too. And he'll do as I say!" The drunk had one hand rested against the wall, the other attempting to gesture for Tony to come closer to him without any refusal, his face more serious and his eyes locked onto Karen's, hoping to assert dominance once more. Tony didn't budge, partly because of the force of his mother and partly because he didn't want to.

"NOW!" he bellowed, punching a hole through the wall. Tony and Karen bounced back. He started to lose patience, taking a step closer.

"You don't touch him, anymore." Karen tried to back him off with the other arm.

"You wha'? And you think you're going to stop me? Every house has a master, and I'm the master around here."

Karen sensed aggression in her master as he sensed fear in his subjects. "Now, give me him!" He backhanded her to the floor, not knocking her out but strong enough of a strike to give her a bruise.

All Karen could do was just watch as Tony had no way of escaping the clutches of the man. She had to do something before he could hurt her little Tony. He grabbed Tony by the neck of the vest and, with the other hand, was ready to throw a ruthless punch at him. The next moment, Tony stumbled back into the stairs, blood starting to pour from his nose.

Karen screamed.

"HE'S NOT YOUR SON!"

8: NOW

"He struck me, and that's when Mother told him."

"Told him what?" Isabella asked, eager to hear the rest, three cigarettes down.

"That I wasn't his," Tony revealed. "The next moment, Mother left us. Without a reason and never to return." Isabella started to well up with little streaks of tears, putting an arm around her boyfriend's shoulders with care. "I haven't heard from her since, and him downstairs hasn't been able to change his ways."

"I'm so sorry." With her head resting against Tony's broad and mighty shoulder, Isabella spoke with truth. "But why are you still here if he acts like the way he does?"

It was difficult for Tony to spit his words out, stuttering, not wanting to well up himself as he thought it wasn't *manly*. Nevertheless, he carried on telling Bella that deep down, he was grateful that – although he was a lunatic – he had stuck around. Perhaps sympathy, too; perhaps Tony didn't want the man who practically helped raise him to suffer any more than he already had done.

"End of the day..." Tony's sympathetic and soft tone turned aggressive. "He needs me way more than I need him."

"It certainly looks that way," Isabella agreed.

After a moment of silence and thought, a thud began to ascend in volume, like a hungover – most likely still intoxicated – man putting a great deal of effort into walking up the stairs. Isabella gasped at every stomp and crash into the wall.

"Don't worry, he can't do harm. Especially since he's been like this," Tony clarified.

Isabella took a breath of relief and rose with the help of her boyfriend. They kept their eye on the doorway to see if Tony's *guardian* somehow managed to make his way past. The man rubbed his aching head, his short, brown hair spiralling in all sorts of directions. He unconsciously leaned against the door frame, getting a good look at the pair that stood before them.

"W-W-Who's t-t-t-th-th...?" He tried to ask a simple question but failed to formulate the words, with Tony cutting him off.

"This is Isabella." Tony presented his partner to him. With his eyebrows raised – only being able to see a blurred image of a woman's figure standing directly in front of him – he released a ridiculous drunken laugh.

"My condolences," he said. "I'm Tony's fa – I mean, I'm Ben." It was as if Tony had witnessed the invention of a time machine, he stood silent, his mouth as close to the ground as it could go, and his eyes almost popping out of their sockets. He actually spoke without any trouble. And finally, without saying a word, with his head swinging in circles as if it was hanging off his neck by a thread, Ben turned back around and made his way into the comfort of his own room for the first time in weeks. Not wanting to be rude, Isabella held back a snigger.

"It's fine, you know," Tony said, knowing what Isabella was trying not to do. "I just hope he can sort himself out before something dreadful happens." This time, it was Tony's arm that wrapped around Bella's shoulders, although his hand was inching its way down towards her chest. Was this escalating too quickly? Tony didn't think so, but Bella thought differently; she glanced down at his hand, but Tony acted as innocent as possible and tried to brush it off, changing the subject like the past twenty minutes to half an hour didn't happen. "I've got something you may like." Tony led Isabella around the mattress by the wrist and showed her out of his room and into Ben's. Ben was out like a light, half the duvet off the bed and his head dangling off the top corner. This gave Tony the right opportunity to quietly sneak into the drawers that stood at the foot of the bed, unravelled his way through the creased and unsorted piles of clothes until he got to the bottom to reveal to Isabella ripped, skin-tight jeans, a leather jacket, a pair of heels, and a top that revealed the stomach that resembled a bra. "This is kind of like a reminder we keep of Mother," he whispered, handing her the clothes that contrasted with what she originally intend to look like. "And I want you to have them."

"Oh, Tony, what a wonderful gesture, but what about Ben?"

"He won't even notice," Tony said calmly. "Go and put them on. I bet you'll look stunning." Isabella wasn't too keen on this idea, her eyebrow narrowed, looking concerned. She may have had second thoughts. "I promise I won't look." Still a slight uneasy about the idea of changing into another person's clothes, she hesitated to change but did so anyway as Tony gave off an arrogant smirk before turning around to give her some privacy.

9

In her new requested clothes, Isabella pecked Tony on the cheek as he said goodbye and repeatedly reminded her about the party that was going down. She said that she wasn't going to forget, but seemingly forgot why she had run away from school that very same day.

"And are you sure Hannah and Jess can come? I must warn you they are a bit weird," Isabella said cautiously.

"Yes, I've said that is fine," he reminded her, waving it off like it didn't matter. And to Tony, it didn't really matter who came to his party; all he cared about was what he was going to get out of Isabella coming.

"Okay." Isabella then headed onto the street, and then looked back at Tony standing in the doorway. With his bulging eyes unable to move away from the sensational view that was his girlfriend, he gave a flamboyant wave and shut the door behind him, leaving Bella to chuckle at his final actions and walk home with the thought of the party – her first ever party – being mere days away. Yet, the thought of facing her father once again didn't slip into her mind until she arrived back at Chessington Close later that day.

10

Before Bella could even walk through the door, Anthony emerged from the top of the stairs, running down them frantically as if he had super-speed.

"Bella!" he shouted, darting towards her. He tightly wrapped his arms around her, not allowing Isabella to leave his grasp. "I've been worried sick. Where have you been? The school rang me telling me you had run away after students surrounded you when you were on the floor."

"I'm fine, I'm fine, honestly," she said patiently, trying to pacify her overwrought father. "I just wasn't feeling too good," she continued, as if it wasn't such a bad thing that she had skipped most of the school day.

"I thought something had happened, I was going to call the police." And he had the right to. Once the phone rang earlier that day not too long after Isabella had run off, Anthony's immediate thought was to call the police and go out searching. It wasn't like Isabella to run off like that. He had recalled only one other time when she had done that, and that was during the closing moments of Sharron's funeral. Seeing a waterfall of tears rush down Isabella's face was heartbreaking enough, let alone that they were in the front row during the service at the crematorium with the closed casket to be faded away by the closing of those rose-red curtains.

But Anthony didn't want to be bringing up that day during a serious moment like this, which Isabella didn't seem too bothered about. She just brushed everything off, carelessly agreeing to whatever Anthony was saying, in a mind of her own, and the thought of the party still roaming freely.

"Look, I won't do it again, and I'm sorry. There, do you feel better now?" Isabella rolled her eyes and shrugged her shoulders, a smug look appearing on her face.

"Not really," Anthony said firmly, rejecting the apology. He also knew that if he had said that he accepted it, deep down, he would have disbelieved it. *Never tell lies*, he thought. *I would never lie.* "Just disappointed."

"Okay then," Isabella scoffed, pushing away from her dad, brushing off him as she trampled up the stairs, heading to her room.

"Besides, where did you get those clothes?" Anthony pointed out.

There was no reply. Anthony puffed and panted, turning a grape purple. Smoke was about to horn out of his ears. Needing to calm down, he tried to take steady breaths, collapsing onto the couch; imagining Sharron sitting at the end, his head resting on her knee as she gently rubbed his head, humming a soothing tune which he hadn't heard of before.

Anthony blocked out the slam of his daughter's bedroom door, leaving Isabella alone. She chucked herself onto her bed, and stared up at the ceiling and then to the Wall of Wonder. And that's when she acted on the thought. Isabella reached up as far as she could with the extended elevation of the springs in her mattress, found a crease in the wallpaper and tore the Wall of Wonder to shreds.

What in the blazes are you doing?

She blocked out Mother's disappointment, and continued to rip the paper piece by piece.

The past has happened, and Isabella was looking forward to the future. She wasn't going to let her father – someone who didn't know what she was truly going through – spoil her week. *Tony is the only one who knows me*, she thought as she finished letting out her frustrations on the former Wall of Wonder. She saw her future with Tony, and only Tony. Yes, Hannah and Jess were still her friends, sure, but do they really get her, too? *No*, she thought. The party was going to be the turning point in Isabella's life. No more mourning; no more acting like everything is okay. She was going to enjoy life, starting with the session.

Who knew what was going to happen?

Chapter Five

Strike II – The Session

1

It was the day before the party, and it was the first time since they had met that Isabella had bailed on Hannah and Jess. All the pair did was sit in the park, watching pedestrians jog, or walk by with their earphones in, or watching their kids grow up as they rode on their bikes – well, Hannah was. Jess was rummaging through her backpack for more and more snacks.

"You know what's weird? What's weird is that I've bought two four packs of Twix for two quid from Tesco, along with an extra-large of *non*-diet coke for an extra three. But I went into my corner shop and saw the exact same things, but for flipping three pound cheaper. How crazy is that, right? And now I think about if I had just went to the corner shop instead, then what else I could've bought with that extra two pound..."

"I'll tell you what's weird: the way Bella has been acting," admitted Hannah, cutting Jess off.

"... Same with the crisps, too. Squares are cheaper than French Fries. Why? French Fries are *way* nicer." Jess continued to babble on about snacks when there were more important matters to be dealt with.

"Jess?"

"Me being a cheapskate, though, what do I go and do? Buy the Squares instead."

"Jess."

"Oh well, I guess the Squares will do." She finally took a breath. "I need a Twix after all that." She searched her bag, reaching down to the very bottom and pulled out a single Twix bar. Jess smiled from ear to ear, holding the bar up like she had just won a trophy and she wanted to show it off. Hannah couldn't do anything apart from roll her eyes, sigh, and think what made them friends. "There you are, you lovely chocolate stick of deliciousness," Jess complimented the snack, delicately opening the wrapper, getting a whiff of the cocoa and biscuit.

"Jess!" Hannah smacked the bar out of Jess' tight grip, thinking she had actually received her attention in return.

"What'd you do that for?" Jess sighed, but then rekindled in the moment by picking it up from the grass and explaining, "five second rule, Hannah." She was about to take a well-deserved bite, only for Hannah to snatch it once again from her hand and throw it into the bushes on the other side of the footpath.

"Jess, will you shut up for one second?"

"Okay. What's up?" Jess sighed.

"Don't you think that Isabella has been acting awkward recently?" Jess couldn't recall a point when she had the feeling that their friend was acting weird. "I mean..." Hannah continued to explain, "that ever since she's been with Tony, she hasn't been *herself*."

"Ah, yeah. Kind of like how she, for some reason, ran out of the school without warning a few days ago?"

Jess finally caught up, now understanding what Hannah was trying to say.

"Exactly."

"What can we do, though? She's obsessed with this Tony kid, and his party is tomorrow night, so..." Hannah couldn't think of a solution on the spot. "Do you think we should still go?" Jess added.

It had occurred to Hannah just then that on the day that Isabella mentioned the party to them when they were over at hers, Isabella didn't clearly say that she wanted them there; she remembered her only saying that they could come *if they wanted.*

"I think we should, just in case," Hannah defined. A smart decision which they both agreed on. They had decided to stand up and leave, knowing that Isabella wasn't going to show. But then, Hannah put an arm in front of Jess as they began to walk. "Just a thought though, we won't know anyone there. So, I think we should be hesitant."

"Okay." Jess nodded and walked some more alongside Hannah. Most of the time, Jess didn't really know much about her whereabouts, allowing Hannah or Isabella to take the lead on most of their adventures together. But knowing that she could trust them meant just as much to her as their friendship did. Unfortunately, Jess started to have second thoughts on trusting this new Isabella Rose-Eccleby. "Hannah, I don't want Bella not to be our friend after this. You know, just in case she doesn't actually want us there, and we embarrass her."

It was like Jess had read Hannah's mind. Hannah stopped and didn't say a word, but gave a gentle – hesitant – smile; she didn't want to lose Bella either, but after the party, Hannah was dreading having to consider letting one of her oldest and best friends go.

2

It was time, and Isabella was ready to enjoy her life.

She examined herself carefully in the mirror: her hair was tatty, curled like pasta, skin-tight short-shorts exposing three-quarters of her legs, a shaggy white top that only covered the top half of her body, black heels, and a leather jacket to match.

Her phone vibrated, lying on top of her bedside cabinet. Bella picked it up immediately and read the notification; it was a message from her lad.

"Party in fifteen," she read aloud, but quiet enough for her father not to hear. Isabella typed a simple 'Ok' which followed up with a paragraph of kisses.

That's number two, *Isabella*, she could hear. It was the delicate voice of her mother, Sharron, sounding more firm than she could remember. *One more and you're out.* Isabella shook her head rapidly, trying to block the voice out. To keep her mind from continuously blocking Mother's warning, Isabella focused on her untied laces and reached down to double knot them. *One more*, *Bella.* She started to pant, panic, and stuff her face into her pillow that laid on the top of her bed.

"One minute, Bella."

"Shut up," Isabella demanded, tasting the cotton polyester as her teeth dug into the pillow as she spoke.

"What do you mean? I'm only saying, just a minute for dinner." It was Anthony, who said that he had been knocking for two minutes with no response. "And I was hoping we could talk," he continued softly, his voice coming through the closed door and echoing into her ears. Isabella didn't respond, just humming and grunting. "I know we haven't been close recently, but I just want..." He didn't bother replying. From what he was receiving in return, he felt there was no point, and so left her in peace and hung his head in sadness and guilt as he entered the bathroom.

The door closed fully just before Isabella's creaked open slightly. She poked her head through the gap, glancing back and forth, hoping for no sign of Anthony. And when the coast was clear, she made her escape down the stairs and out of the front door. She looked back, holding the grand door open, listening out for the chain to flush, and when it did, she made a run for it.

"I'm not Daddy's little girl anymore," she declared just before the door slammed shut behind her.

"Isabella, did you say something?" he asked, thinking he had heard her, shutting the door behind. "Bella?" He searched around the landing, all rooms, downstairs. Nowhere.

Before he could have the chance to tell her that he was sorry, sorry for everything and for what had happened that night, and that he wished he could've done more as a father, Isabella Rose-Eccleby was gone.

Both from the house and as a person.

3

Tony's party was ready to get underway, but nobody had arrived apart from Hannah and Jess. They walked up towards the front door, hesitant to knock as the thought of some random elder opening the door

– realising that they had the wrong house – slipped their minds.

"I don't know about this," Jess whispered, her fingernails digging deep into Hannah's shoulder. They stopped and Hannah looked at her seriously.

"Come on," Hannah replied. "This might even be good," she added, prompting Jess to walk up with her instead of turning around and backing out at the last possible moment. Hannah linked arms with her uncomfortable friend and led her to the front door. Yes, they made it. They could hear the music blasting through the walls, and a bit of them had hoped – even Hannah – that Tony (the boyfriend of Isabella that they hadn't even met yet) wouldn't be able to hear the tap on the door. Would he be everything that she made him out to be? Was he good to her? Or was he someone who treated her with no respect and she wasn't telling them? All these questions without confirmed answers. As her friends, and more importantly, her safety, Hannah and Jess prayed to God that it was the first.

Hannah took the lead and clenched her fist, took a deep breath in unison to Jess, and finally… Like if it was a cue, a tall, broad man opened the door and stared at them like a bouncer of a nightclub.

"Ah, you must be Isabella's friends," he said gleefully, smiling unconvincingly. "Come in. Come in." Tony Lesterson allowed them in. He wasn't himself either, dressing up as smart as he could: an unironed, black shirt, stained jeans, and shoes with clear holes at the toe in which he clearly did a bad attempt at sewing it up – breaking instantly. He stood up straight in front of them; like a cleaner of a hotel waiting for a tip, Tony waited for a compliment on the use of decorations that he had placed – on his own, as if it was an achievement– around the house: one party banner and a number of balloons.

"Erm... Nice place you've got," lied Jess. *You can't polish a turd*, is what she wanted to say, but she thought that would be rude.

"Aw, thank you," said Tony, his hands on his heart, appearing to appreciate the phony compliment too much. The *first* two guests laughed awkwardly as the host gestured for them to sit down in the lounge. "I'll get some refreshments as you two get settled and await the others. Take a seat." He bowed and left for the kitchen.

"This isn't right," Jess reminded Hannah, flapping the misty air away from her face.

Hannah hated to admit that she was now having second thoughts. Another look around the lounge, and it had knocked her sick. Her stomach turned, shook her head, and aggressively pulled Jess up with her and entered the next room in which Tony was pouring two cups of *juice*.

"Tony?" Hannah caught his attention, he turned with the plastic cups in hand, presented the pair with their beverages. "Thank you, but I think we're just going to leave."

"Leave? But you've just got here," Tony implied. Hannah and Jess placed both of their drinks into the filthy sink, and moved back into the hall with Tony following.

"I know," Jess joined, but then forced Hannah and herself to stop. Her eyes were wide; even Hannah hadn't even seen her that stunned before.

"What's wrong?" Tony asked, grinning, and tilting his head on an angle.

Jess rapidly nudged Hannah in the stomach until Hannah caught what Jess noticed: in the corner of the lounge, aside the television, was crates of alcohol. Hannah winced in fear and put her hand over her mouth, gasping. They had backed up all the way to the front door by this point.

"Well, Isabella obviously doesn't want us here." Hannah spoke firmly, no fear anymore. "We'll get out of your way. Enjoy your party," she snarled, finding the door handle, and pushing Jess outside in front of her, slamming the door after her.

Tony just stood there, staring straight at where they had just stood, not saying a word but they suddenly started to laugh uncontrollably. He had to catch his breath before he could alert everyone who hid upstairs that it was all clear to come down. A tsunami of party guests tumbled over one another as they ran down the stairs.

"I thought they would never leave," one girl said in between gulps of beer.

"Now we can really get the party started," a boy cheered, patting Tony on the back. The rest of the crowd whooped and cheered along with him, amping up the music and ripping open the many crates of beer, wine, vodka, gin, and whisky. You name it, Tony had it.

"Why did you even invite them?" another girl, obviously intrigued by what she saw in front of her, said to Tony. She didn't take it any further, though, as she unfortunately knew that he was taken. And at the moment, Isabella Rose-Eccleby came walking down the stairs, proud.

"Because if I didn't, they would've made me feel really shitty. But hey, I knew they wouldn't last long,"

Isabella sneered with a confident smirk, bursting out into laughter, being handed a bottle of her first ever beer, ready to enjoy the night and the rest of her life.

That's strike two, Isabella. Three strikes and you're out.

4

They partied through the night well into the early hours of the morning, the deafening music still shaking the house at half past two in the morning. Tony obviously hadn't heard of neighbours.

A few guests had left before midnight, but from first glance at the crowd that piled into the Lesterson household, you wouldn't think anyone did. It was tough to squeeze through the other party guests, but Isabella – who had four vodka shots by this point – finally made her way passed to find her boyfriend, not without tumbling over her own feet though.

Tony was in the kitchen, chatting with a small group of people who looked around a similar age.

"Tony!" she shouted, getting the group's attention, falling into one of them as she joined the circle. "Hiii!"

"Bella," Tony said, flicking his head up and winking at her, acting all cool in front of his mates. If Isabella was sober enough to comprehend where she even was and what time she was up till, then this attitude from Tony would have been questionable. "You enjoying yourself?"

"Are you kidding?" she laughed, tumbling into Tony now, swinging her arm around his shoulder. "This is the best night of my life." The drunk sixteen-year-old whipped her head round and gazed at what one of

Tony's friends had in their possession. "This alcoholic?" The friend looked at her as if she was stupid.

"Yeah," he said cautiously. And without warning, the drink was snatched out of his hand and being chugged by Isabella, everyone swarming around her cheering, clapping, and laughing proudly.

"Chug! Chug! Chug! Chug! Chug!" the sea of her new fans chanted until she had completely downed the drink, haughtily smashing the bottle on the ground. The crowd whooped and cheered her on. "Bella! Bella! Bella!" They patted her back, high-fived her, and appreciated her for her so-called accomplishment, all whilst Tony gazed around thinking.

This could be my moment to strike, he thought.

Tony, who wasn't too drunk but merry, backed Isabella's audience up, giving her room.

"Let's give it up for Isabella!" he proclaimed, raising her hand in victory. He turned to her, her eyes fading away and rolling into the back of her head. "Now, you said that this was the best night of your life, right?" She nodded and he turned back to the audience. "How about I make your night even better?" he asked arrogantly. The men of the party cheered him on, raising whatever drink they had in their hand for him.

And so, he manoeuvred Isabella and himself into the hallway past the crowd, who carried on with the party as the couple went upstairs for some privacy. He held her hand passionately, leading her up the stairs, making sure she didn't pass out or fall over. With an evil grin on his face, he opened his bedroom door gentleman-like. He watched her bounce off the walls and tip over, Tony's mattress saving her from a possible concussion; either way, Tony expected Isabella to forget this night.

"Wh... What are we doing up here?" she mumbled. She spun her head round and round clockwise, gazing around his bedroom. *Strike two*, *Isabella*, she heard again; this time seemed louder, her ears ringing. "Stop it," she said under her breath.

"What?" Tony stood there at the end of the mattress, confused. "I haven't done anything." He shrugged.

He hadn't done anything... *Yet*.

Strike two! *Strike two*! The phrase ascended in volume. Isabella covered her ears and backed up against the wall, her eyes ghostly, blank, and showing no emotion. Tony, however, sought a desire to become the true dominant one of the couple. He was the man after all; the men always have control in a sexual relationship, don't they?

Tony Lesterson dropped to his hands and knees, and pounced onto the mattress, his eyes evil like Satan. He didn't lose focus and didn't hold anything back. Tony crawled towards the defenceless girl, who was still hearing the voice, like a multi-legged creature feasting on its prey.

Nose-to-nose, the voice of Sharron suddenly stopped and Isabella snapped back into reality. Tony's eyes locked onto hers and out came that smug grin, his rotting teeth showing.

"Tony, what are you doing?" she whispered, breaking eye contact as she peered down.

"Don't worry about it. Everything is going to be alright," Tony bluffed, like a lightning bolt – from out of nowhere – grabbing at her by the heels and dragging her to the centre of the mattress. She was trapped, nowhere to go, glaring at the dominant predator that was Tony, unbuttoning his shirt.

"Wait..." Isabella held up her hand to block the sight she saw.

"If you don't make a fuss, this will be a whole lot easier," he advised, forcefully putting her arm back down.

She wanted to scream, but her body wouldn't allow it. It felt like the world had stopped spinning and the planets had aligned, like an ancient prophecy coming true.

From downstairs, nobody could hear her plead for help and for Tony to stop – revealing his true intentions. She wept helplessly, her tears like waterfalls. Her begging couldn't stop the storm that was brewing.

"If you really loved me, you would do this for me."

And from that single sentence, Isabella Rose-Eccleby's fate had been sealed.

Chapter Six

Isabella's Vision

1

Not by persuasion, but by having to resort to nipping and biting, Isabella finally managed to escape the wrath of Tony Lesterson.

She grabbed her coat and made her way down the stairs, without consideration, pushing whoever was in her vision out of the way. Bella left, yet Tony did not go after her. Self-conscious, Isabella imagined that the guests had been in on what had occurred between her and Tony, making out little sounds of laughter as she left the party and walked into the pouring rain on her own. Isolated as she was, her jacket unable to keep her warm, and without a hood, her hair had been soaked as thunder clashed and lightning struck.

Knowing that there were no cars on the road, Isabella walked in the centre; she felt some sort of comfort from it. Her arms were folded, her legs unsteady, and the feeling of collapsing in the middle of the road she felt was almost upon her. Just in time, Isabella made her way through the back alleys of the neighbourhood, getting leverage from the upright walls on both sides as she passed homeless men and women with yellow teeth

– the remaining teeth, that is – that only had rags for clothing.

Is this my fate? Isabella thought. She couldn't bear to face her father, which meant she had nowhere to go and, most importantly, no one; Hannah and Jess weren't options anymore, regretfully recalling that she had chosen a party over them. The guilt started to kick in; it was a time when she needed someone, anyone, but she had no one. No person alive would understand her situation.

No person *alive*.

2

Did Isabella really have a choice? She had decided to go to the place where she felt most warm and welcome: her mother's grave. The cemetery didn't open until six that morning, but that wasn't going to stop Isabella from scaling the wall into the resting place of some of Castlehead's most beloved citizens – Sharron included.

Bella stumbled across the grave site, starting to groan at what she would soon figure out was the suffering of a hangover. She needed a place to rest and Sharron's memorial bench was the place. The suffering girl made her way up the long stretch of concrete until she turned off to where her mother lay.

Isabella crumbled onto the bench, all damp and soggy. She yawned and used one of the bench's arms as support for her jacket which she used as a substitute pillow. Although the storm had died down by this point, the wind whistled aggressively. The girl hadn't fallen completely asleep yet, the sight of her mother's grave stopping her. She tossed and turned, but there was no way for Isabella to get comfortable.

Half an hour had passed and the sun had started to steadily rise. Disturbing Isabella from her lacklustre slumber, another whistle flowed gently through the air and into Isabella's ears – though, this time, it wasn't the wind. It had caused Isabella to rise, head banging, and look at Sharron's grave. Her eyes were barely open, her vision fuzzy; unable to make out the blue silhouette of a woman walking towards her.

"Mother?" Isabella rubbed her eyes to make sure that this was truly happening before her.

Sharron didn't say a word, only responding with a confirming nod. Mother extended a hand and the touch felt so real; so real that Isabella welled up with tears and smiled. She then rose, looking at her mother dead in the eye. She was exactly how Isabella remembered her. Sharron, on the other hand, smiled back at her, happily shocked.

You have grown so much, Isabella heard Mother say in the same soothing tone she always spoke in. Sharron grabbed both of her daughter's hands delicately, and led her out of the cemetery towards a place where they both held dear to their hearts: Wardle Gardens.

3

Isabella didn't need to ask where her mother was taking her. Her instinct had told her. It felt like she was six all over again when Bella walked along Wardle Street, recalling that every house on the street had its own name (Wardle Gardens, Wardle Palace, even Wardle Heart). Bewitched by the street's appearance, Isabella saw the street the way it was before Sharron's horrific death: bright, colourful, and full of life. But what

Isabella really walked along was a street with piles of wood, brick, and stone – except for a couple of houses that still stood, yet was on the verge of being dismantled for reconstruction. A graveyard for houses.

At the end of the narrow street still stood Wardle Gardens. The pair glared at the house which they once lived in, and Isabella suddenly started to feel warm. The warmth she had felt back when the Rose-Eccleby family lived there. *I am home*, she thought, and stopped and knew that she wanted to hop over the gate and sprint towards her home without stopping…

But Sharron wouldn't allow her.

Sweetheart, don't be fooled by its homely appearance, Bella heard Sharron warn her. *It's not all what it seems*. What did Sharron Rose mean by that? Isabella didn't believe what she was saying. She was home and home is where the heart is.

"I am home," she replied.

There are things that you don't know.

The warm feeling she had felt had suddenly gone away, replaced with a cold, trembling shiver that shot down through her spine. The tingling returned. Every inch of her was trembling, but not from the wind. Something seemed off about Wardle Gardens now; it didn't look like it did when she was there. It was new now, fresh, the walls matched the door with snow-white paint freshly covered all over the bricks.

The night had turned into day, and Isabella leaned forward, squinting, getting a better view of the door handle wriggling. Someone was unlocking the door, but it wasn't clear whether it was from the inside or from the outside.

"Come on, come on!" a familiar voice said.

"I'm trying, I'm trying!" another familiar voice replied.

Both of the voices seemed to sound excited. Isabella then heard the unlocking of the door.

"Wait a minute..." Isabella said, unaware that her mother wasn't next to her, or as a blue silhouette. She was at the door, alive and in person, next to the man who held the keys.

"Come on, Anthony."

4: THEN

Fresh out of purchasing the Wardle Gardens property, Anthony Eccleby and Sharron Rose leaped into their new home, hugging, and smooching one another.

The house wasn't what they envisioned at first, but with paint, hammers, and wallpaper, it would be everything they had wanted. Anthony and Sharron stood in the hallway, getting a look at the wallpaper that needed to be removed, and the floorboards that still needed to be carpeted. Anthony took off his jacket and flung in onto the bottom step of the staircase. He peered up the stairs, getting a look at the top where the stairs split off into two: the left heading into the bathroom, and the right leading onto the landing. The landing was wide enough to fit three people in a row and was shaped like a hexagon.

"We need a banister," said Sharron, leading the way up the stairs and noticing that there was no banister attached to the wall. They stood in the middle of the stair junction.

"Did we really need to buy a four-bedroom house?" asked Anthony, staring at the four closed doors surrounding the landing.

The floorboards creaked but were able to take their weight – just – as they opened the doors one by one to reveal four decent-sized bedrooms. Although the rooms were empty and looked similar, the couple knew which room was going to be theirs and which one was going to be young Isabella's – who was being taken care of by Sharron's unwell father.

"We can make one an office if you work from home, dear," Sharron suggested, taking Anthony by the mucky hand, and showing him the room closest to the right of them. Anthony stroked his chin and agreed to the idea.

"This one can just be the spare room, yeah?" Anthony pointed at the room opposite them. Sharron nodded. "And this one will be ours?" Anthony walked into the room next door to them and envisioned what the room would look like. Standing behind him, Sharron softly rubbed his shoulders as she placed her chin on one of them.

"We've done well," she said proudly. Anthony sighed, hanging his head. "Look, I know Mother wasn't happy with us getting together, and it has been hard since she passed, but this is the start of something new. The start of a new chapter in our lives, Anthony." She squeezed passed him and entered their bedroom herself, placed a firm grip on his hands and dragged him across the room like teaching someone how to ice skate, trying her best to take her husband's mind off her mother degrading him for his upbringing.

It partly worked, as they laughed back down the stairs to reveal the lounge. It was big, and this was the room

Sharron knew she would have full control over. Making their way through the lounge and a door at the other end, they entered the kitchen. It was more long than wide and to the left of the door was a built-in cupboard for cleaning utensils and tools. Opposite the cupboard was another small room the size of a porta-potty. It was a downstairs toilet. Anthony jokily thought that if they had two toilets they would be moving up in society.

And at the far end of the kitchen was the back door. It was heavy and cracked to pieces, causing more strain on whoever tried to open it. At first, it took both of them to pull down on the handle and get it to open, and when they did, they saw themselves in an extension. Windows surrounded them, but the temperature was freezing; Sharron suggested the first thing they would attempt to do was try and get some heating into this room, not to mention that the shockingly cold marble tiles added insult to injury. From the front of the house, this extension wasn't visible as the newly built garage that Sharron's father built as a surprise blocked it.

"It needs work, but we'll manage," said Anthony hopefully, making their way back out to the front to get another good view at what they had just purchased.

They kissed as a congratulations to one another for all the effort and hard work they had put into buying the house that they had always wanted.

Abruptly, Sharron backed away from the kiss and jerked her head as if she was trying to get something out of her ear.

"What?" Sharron said under her breath. "No. You're wrong," she added rudely.

Anthony, thinking she was talking to him, snapped, "What?"

Sharron shook her head again, remembering where she was.

"Huh? Oh, nothing, Eccleby. Just..." She tried to think of something which didn't make her seem like she was going crazy. "Just lost in the moment, that's all."

"Okay, then." Anthony gave her that smug look that always made her laugh and act like she was blushing. She saved herself, wanting to brush what she had heard away before they went back to taking their new home in. But she couldn't.

You're not winning, girl. I warned you about him. One of you will go sooner or later.

Knowing it was the voice of her mother, Sharron had swept it under the carpet and acted like she had never heard the voice before. Deep down, though, Sharron Rose also knew the reason why her mother may have been coming back to her in recent times.

5

Brenda Rose was a witch of a woman. She had bushy grey hair and black eyes that resembled small tunnels. Her skin was wrinkly, wrinklier than any other seventy-five-year-old woman; close friends and relatives called her – behind her back of course – the Prehistoric Witch. Her cackle was evil, and she wore long black dresses, like the dress one might wear at a funeral, but she never attended funerals. She wore these dresses for fun. Brenda's presence would suck all the fun out of an atmosphere, and no matter how wrong she was, Brenda believed in her dark, bitter soul that she was always right.

Always right.

Sharron's home down on Eccose had been in the Rose family for three generations until she moved out for Wardle Gardens. This – along with the idea of courting Anthony overall – didn't sit well with Brenda; even her father wasn't impressed.

Not too long after Anthony and Sharron first started courting, Sharron constantly warned him about her parents and how unsupportive they had been during their brief relationship. Anthony, not always taking it seriously, just replied telling her to take it easy and how it was going to be okay. How wrong he was.

On the first official meeting between boyfriend and future in-laws, Brenda immediately criticised him for his lowlife demeanour and lack of education, even though Anthony had politely informed Sharron's parents that he was working full-time as a junior builder, working on refurbishing Fellmarsh Station.

"Yeah... whatever," Brenda snarled, dismissing Anthony's accomplishments within the workplace.

"Mum!" Sharron yelled, warning her mother to not push it, giving her a stern look. It was like looking in a mirror.

Sharron's Eccose home was twice as large as Anthony's. He lived on the rough end of Castlehead, but had a heart of gold. The room that they sat in whilst having Indian cuisine, a type of food Anthony only had on special occasions, such as his birthday the year before, was the lounge. It was double the size of any ordinary sitting room. Just like the rest of the houses on Eccose Street, you would enter the lounge straight away once opening the front door. In the far left corner of the room was the smooth, wooden staircase that spiralled up to the landing where you had the choice of four doors – three which lead to bedrooms, and the other to the bathroom in which Brenda had installed a shower as soon as the house was officially hers.

"I must say that this dinner is rather lovely, ma'am," Anthony said, complimenting her on his dinner.

"Actually, it was my husband that made it," Brenda sneered.

"Oh, sorry, sir." He continued eating the lamb bhuna, still amazed at the house that he was sitting in.

After dinner, Brenda kindly took her husband and daughter's plates, but snatched Anthony's, and took them into the kitchen to be washed.

"Can I see you for a moment?" Brenda wasn't asking Sharron to follow her into the kitchen, she was demanding, leaving Anthony and her husband, Harold, to uncomfortably make small talk whilst the girls chatted away. "You like this one, then?" asked Brenda, carelessly putting the dirty dishes into the sink.

"I do, I really do," Sharron said honestly. Brenda scoffed and turned the tap until the water turned warm, squirted some washing-up liquid in and waited for the bubbles to show. "And I hope you can, too."

"Hope?" snapped Brenda. "Hope? I hoped for you to be courting someone like us, not one of *him*." She stopped with the washing, turning her full attention to her daughter, who she thought was acting disobediently. "Whatever happened to Jonathan Q?"

"He was stubborn and too patriarchal," Sharron explained. Jonathan Q was Sharron's partner for only a month not too long before she met Anthony. He was nice and everything, she went on to say, but she didn't want to be treated like an object by someone who she saw just as equal.

"Darling, that's how relationships are. Me and Daddy were exactly how a couple should be." Sharron wanted to argue back and say that times had changed and if she were to court someone, she wanted it to be for love, not for the patriarchal society which Castlehead was still in. "Sweetheart..." Brenda kneeled down to Sharron's level and continued saying, "you'll realise one day that this one isn't the right one for you. And you'll see long after I'm gone that I was right all along."

Sharron had just brushed it off as one of those *parentisms* where your parents think they're telling you the right stuff, and then you, as the child, go out and prove them wrong. And that's exactly what Sharron set out to do.

6

Their relationship had many ups and not so many downs. Two years had passed and, by then, they had become hopelessly devoted to each other. For Sharron's eighteenth, three years before the millennium, Anthony surprised her with a trip down south to London for the weekend. He had planned the entire trip and had sorted out exact dates and times for when they would be seeing the famous London sights: Big Ben, the London Eye, and Buckingham Palace, just to name a few.

The idea sprung to mind after a day out at the fair the previous summer; Sharron had walked through a spinning tunnel of the world's most famous landmarks and briefly mentioned she would love to at least see one of them. Even Brenda and Harold had to admit that it was a good present – brilliant, in fact. The accommodation had been paid for and everything. And then, for her twenty-first, the proposal.

"Yes," she squeaked through happy tears during a luxury dinner at where they had their first date, Cheryl's Italian. The staff and other restaurant guests clapped and cheered for such a glorious moment. The ring sparkled in the moonlight; silver with microscopic diamonds scattered all around.

Of course, Brenda and Harold were furious and had actually thrown up at the news. Their main query was how Anthony had the money to purchase a ring that beautiful?

"Ah, Mrs Rose." Anthony spoke with confidence. "The key is to save up." Nothing else was said and he walked out proudly, hand in hand with his future wife.

Unfortunately, it wasn't all smooth sailing for the Rose-Eccleby family.

Their initial honeymoon plan was to spend two weeks in the sunny Caribbean, a holiday of love and romance. But their time had been cut short once Sharron had received the phone call that would change her life forever.

It was midday and the sun was directly above them as they lay on a pair of sunbeds on the shore of the island, letting the sun roast their skin until they were golden brown, like two loaves of freshly baked bread.

"Excuse me," said a sweaty, skinny Caribbean man in black shorts and a black polo. He was an employee at the five-star hotel that they were staying at. The hotel was built on the shore, only a five-minute walk from where Anthony and Sharron had been laying. "Are you the *Rose-Eccleby* couple?" His English wasn't fluent, but he tried his best.

"Yes," Sharron confirmed, removing her sunglasses to get a better look at the boy, sitting up. "Is there a problem?"

"Erm... No. No problem. You see, there is a – err." The worker was unable to pronounce what he was trying to say, so he swung around to the front of the sunbeds and tried to get it out by gesturing what he meant with his hands.

"There's a message for us?" Anthony guessed.

"Yes. Yes. You must come quick."

The couple stared at each other, wondering what the problem was. They shrugged their shoulders together and followed the hotel employee through the swaying palm trees and into the exotic hotel.

With the employee still leading the way, Sharron and Anthony had been taken to the reception desk where another employee stood holding out the phone that was attached to the wall from behind the bamboo desk. She grunted as Sharron took the phone from her, quickly bowing her head as a way to say thank you.

"Hello?" Sharron said formally. Anthony could vaguely make out what the voice on the other side was saying.

"Is this Mrs Sharron Rose-Eccleby?" It was the voice of a very formal man who tried his best not to sound worried for her.

"Yes, this is she."

"My name is Doctor Emmett Goldstein from the Oak Castle Hospital in Castlehead, and I am sorry to say that your mother, Brenda Rose, has been brought to us in a serious condition." Sharron gasped, unable to find the right words to reply. Sharron tightly grabbed her husband's hand. "Ma'am, are you there?"

"What? Oh, yes. I'm still here," she stuttered, releasing the grip she had on her husband's hand and firmly grasping the telephone with both hands, unknowingly squeezing with all her might. The employees around her – and Anthony, too – thought she might actually break it. Sharron allowed the doctor to give her more information on the situation that they were now in, and kindly asked her if there was any way for her and her husband to get back to Castlehead as soon as possible. "Yes, of course. We'll be on the next flight out. Thank you."

"I'll book the flights, you pack," Anthony suggested knowingly, even without being told about the situation.

Sharron left the phone hanging on its cord and ran as fast as she could up the sturdy wooden stairs up to the second floor where their room was.

"Come on, stay with us, Mother," she kept repeating to herself as she piled everything carelessly into the suitcases that they had brought with them. "Stop, I need you to stay with me," she pleaded, blocking out the hissing, witchy voice of Brenda.

If you had just listened.

7

It was between getting a direct flight from their honeymoon spot to Castlehead International in forty-eight hours, or getting a flight that night that stopped at Heathrow, meaning they would have to switch. But the latter was for that night. They weren't going to take any chances, they had to get home before it was too late.

Their flight to Heathrow in London departed at seven that evening, meaning that they wouldn't arrive back in Castlehead until early morning the next day. Sharron's constant worrying kept them both awake during the duration of both flights, Anthony's main concern being his wife's state of mind – not his mother-in-law's health. He wasn't heartless, but thought that this *emergency* had been over exaggerated, though he didn't say that to Sharron as he knew it would just cause more problems between them two.

Jet-lagged and desperate for a pillow to rest on, the pair of flights had worn Anthony and Sharron out, and, after twelve long, sleepless hours, they had eventually made it back to Castlehead.

They jumped into the first taxi they saw parked outside the airport and told the driver to put his foot down whilst they chucked their luggage in the back seat with them, not wanting to waste any more time by faffing around trying to put them in the boot.

Scared stiff, the driver thought she was going to get pulled over by the police because of how fast she was forced to go on the motorway.

"I'm already going over the limit," she alerted, not taking her eyes off the road, her hands on the wheel at ten and two, her chin almost touching the top as she squinted and concentrated.

"I don't care," Sharron said, uninhibited. "My mother has been rushed into hospital whilst we've been away." Without saying it directly, Sharron hoped that this guilt tripping would make the driver go even faster.

The sun had started to shine through the detached houses and buildings when Sharron and Anthony had finally arrived at Oak Castle Hospital. Rushing, Sharron overpaid the driver and didn't bother accepting the change the driver had offered. She slammed the car door behind her and rushed to the hospital entrance where she met the doctor who she had spoken to over the phone, leaving Anthony to struggle with all the bags.

Doctor Emmett Goldstein looked older than he was, of average height, and in his required uniform. He stood at the entrance since he had received the message that the Rose-Eccleby's were on their way from Castlehead International.

"She's in the West Wing," he said, leading the way through the maze of hospital hallways that smelled like several people had died. They had passed rooms that had people resting, people looking better than they had done when they first arrived, and people who had visiting family members and friends. "Your mother is through here." He stopped in front of a heavy, green door. Sharron and Anthony couldn't hear any noise coming from within the room, blocking out the other screams of pain that could be heard from the rooms around. Anthony placed their luggage next to the door and held his wife's hand, reminding her that he made a vow to be with her through everything and he would never leave go. "Though, I must warn you: you may get a shock."

"I'm ready," she said, uncertain. She inhaled hope and exhaled pain, timidly awaiting the image that she may have to endure when Doctor Goldstein opened the door. Sharron started to go white as a sheet of paper.

"Are you sure?" Doctor Goldstein asked, reassuring that she would be able to handle the next few moments. She nodded and signalled for him to open the door. The door creaked open and the room was small. The first thing that Sharron's eyes caught was the sight of her mother, Brenda Rose, lying in a hospital bed almost lifeless.

There were two other doctors in the room standing up next to the head of the bed and the life-support machines. One doctor had a clipboard and, to Sharron, looked like she was assessing Brenda's health. The other checked her blood pressure and followed up by injecting morphine into her system. From looking at her, you would think that she seemed okay, but she was in excruciating pain; she was skinny, skinny enough to almost make out the bones in her body. Her lips were a ghostly white and she was hardly breathing.

Although Sharron didn't want to admit it at the time, she, along with everyone in the room, including Harold who sat in the corner scared for his wife, knew that Brenda wasn't coming home.

The doctors came up to Sharron and Anthony, trying not to disturb Brenda.

"How did this happen?" Sharron asked suddenly, knowing there was no point beating around the bush.

"She's in serious pain, Mrs Rose," the doctor with the clipboard said. "She won't be coming home." Sharron hugged Anthony with all her might, her face pressed against Anthony's shoulder, tears flowing non-stop like constant waterfalls. "I'll give you all a minute on your own." All three doctors left and did just that.

Sharron slid down beside the bed, taking Brenda's numb, pale hand without her even knowing until a moment later when she struggled to turn her head sideways and open her beady little eyes, squinting although Sharron was directly in front of her almost nose-to-nose.

"S-Sharron?" Brenda gasped. Her body didn't allow her to turn completely over, only having the power to blink and let out little bursts of words at a time. Sharron didn't even know who the woman lying in front of her was. "What are you doing here?" she whispered.

"You didn't think I wasn't going to come back, did you?" she asked rhetorically. Brenda couldn't reply, gasping for oxygen. Brenda let out a slight smile as Harold held their daughter close, the sight of her family with her for her final moments reminding her how lucky she was to have them both in her life. But then, Anthony came into view. The smile had vanished and was replaced with a snarl, full of pure hatred and bitterness.

"S-Someday, someday..." Brenda struggled to speak but used all of her remaining strength to finish the sentence. "Someday, Sharron, y-you'll real-ise th-that I was..." Her voice started to fade. "That I was..." She was what?

"You were what, Mother?" Sharron urged. "What?!" Sharron started to tremble and panic; her voice broke and had restarted to well up with more tears. But it was when Brenda didn't reply and her eyes were peacefully closed that she had come to the inevitable realisation that her mother, Brenda Rose, was now resting in peace.

The taxi-ride home a number of hours later was silent, no words had been said and their feelings weren't heard but each one of them knew how they were feeling. That night, no one, except Anthony, had any sleep. Sharron just laid there in her bed with a snoring Anthony, glaring at the ceiling thinking about what had occurred and if her mother's death had truly hit her yet.

8

However, although that was a good number of years before Sharron and Anthony had welcomed their gorgeous baby girl, Isabella Rose-Eccleby, into the world and before their purchase of Wardle Gardens, the voice of Brenda Rose would suddenly appear in the mind of Sharron at the happiest of moments.

Wardle Gardens started to feel more homely once all of their newly bought furniture had been fitted, and carpets had been added along with the stripping of the old wallpaper which had been replaced with fresh new rolls.

And regardless of the repetitive days of getting up, working, helping with homework, cleaning, making dinner, going back to sleep, and doing it all over again the next day – to Sharron – it was home. Learning to temper the hearing of her mother's voice, Sharron reminded herself of times of happiness and pushed away the memories of her mother scolding her. But then, she didn't just start to hear Brenda; she started to see her, too.

The visions had started a week after Isabella's sixth birthday. They had thrown a party for her, yet Sharron didn't feel well enough to do what they originally planned: have a birthday party at the soft play centre. But Isabella, with her kind heart, said that she would rather spend a birthday with just her parents than a bunch of classmates who she barely spoke to. It had been another peaceful evening in the Rose-Eccleby household when the visions had begun, Sharron had tucked Isabella into bed, Anthony was downstairs watching the television.

Alone in the queen-sized bed, she stared up at the ceiling motionless, tired but unable to doze off into her slumber. Sharron placed herself dead centre of the bed, knowing that Anthony wouldn't be up for another couple of hours before scooching her over without disturbing her from sleeping. The ceiling seemed to be higher than normal. And damp.

Sharron, tilting her head and squinting, noticed the abnormality of the dampness started to expand across the ceiling and drops of water dripping onto her forehead.

Plink, plink, plink...

She laid awake for as long as she could before she started to try and force herself to fall asleep. Anthony had come up by this point, and seemed concerned for his wife as she described the plinking of the water that fell from the ceiling. He analysed her concerns of the ceiling, although confirming that the ceiling wasn't damp and no dripping was occurring.

Two o'clock in the morning and the dripping still hadn't stopped. Sharron shoved her head under the pillow, weeping silently just wanting to at least get a few hours of sleep. With her head still under the pillow, Sharron felt around the top of the pillow for any more water, but it appeared to stop. She removed her head from the claustrophobic area between the mattress and the pillow, and risked seeing if the ceiling had stopped dripping with water. She sat up and, yep, there was no water. No damp ceiling. No plinking. But what she did see must have been her imagination...

She saw Brenda Rose.

At the edge of Sharron's bed, Anthony out cold, a white silhouette of Sharron's mother stood motionless, only reaching out for her daughter, mouthing the words *in the end, I'll be right*. Brenda's voice started to raise as she managed to slowly make her way around the bed and stand in front of Sharron. Every step Brenda made,

Sharron shuffled back as far as she could in terror. Sharron covered her mouth, wanting to scream but was in so much shock she couldn't. She then felt the skin of her mother's soft hand go through her arm, as if trying to calm her down.

"You know what to do," said Brenda faintly.

Do what? Sharron thought,

"*What*?" Sharron finally whispered, double checking on Anthony. Brenda's silhouette nodded as if to telepathically tell her daughter that she should end *it* by doing the one thing that would make her mother right. "*No*." Sharron had received the message, gasping at her mother's eager look. They both looked down at Anthony snoring away. "I can't."

Brenda leaned in, taking a hold of her daughter's hand. Sharron felt something in her hand – and it wasn't her mother's palm; although she couldn't see it, it felt more like something sharp at the tip and metal.

"Do it," Brenda ordered, her lips almost touching Sharron's ear lobe. "Do it. Do it. Do it." Every time Brenda repeated the demand, Sharron tried to block it out, trying to go back to sleep, stuffing her face in the pillow (with what felt like a blade still in her hand). "You can't ignore the definite reality that I've been right all along," Brenda added, over her daughter. "Sharron. Sharron. Sharron. *Sharron*?"

"Sharron?"

Sharron woke up to the sound of Anthony's high-pitched voice, waking up on top of Anthony with a knife uncontrollably at his neck.

"Anthony?" Sharron said, reassuring where she was, backing away.

"W-What are you doing?" Anthony backed away as far as he could, scared.

Sharron flung the blade onto the floor, the blade of the knife sticking out of the floor. There was silence for a moment, and for once in his life, Anthony had feared his wife.

"I-I think s-something's wrong," Sharron stuttered, her face in her palm, wanting to cry in anger.

"You think?" her husband shouted. "You just had a friggin' blade to my neck!" Sharron gasped as Anthony cursed, hoping to hush him up as she didn't want Isabella hearing. After a moment of reconciling and making sure that Sharron didn't have a *nightmare* like that again, the couple went back to lying down in opposite directions, not looking at one another – Anthony concerned, but Sharron afraid.

Wanting this nightmare to end, Sharron cried herself back to sleep. *You were so close.* Sharron shut her eyes as tight as she could.

There was no doubt that the atmosphere was awkward for all three of them the next morning, even Isabella asked what the shouting was about. Sharron and Anthony *stretched the truth* and assured that nothing was wrong.

"Just a bad dream, that's all."

Isabella said nothing and went straight back to finishing off her drawing of Wardle Gardens – *her* home – and the three of them smiling in front of it. The drawing had been completed by that evening, Isabella's parents proud of her project that made them remember how close they can be and how much of a loving family they could be.

"Hey," Anthony called, getting his daughter and wife's attention. "How about next week we go to the beach?" Isabella jumped up and down with glee, cheering and running around like crazy at this idea. She loved the beach. All of them did.

What a great way to spend my birthday.

Chapter Seven

Home is Where the Heart is

1

Sharron celebrated her birthday as usual on the 5th March, with Anthony and Isabella. Knowing that they had the plan to go to the beach the next day, the family had arranged to have a nice, chill day with films, popcorn, and – of course – birthday cake.

Isabella and Sharron had woken up to the sound of an air horn that Anthony honked at precisely half-eight that morning. And to Sharron's surprise, there was no ghostly body of her mother, but a bunch of roses and a bottle of exquisite champagne. Mother and Daughter walked down the stairs, side-by-side, hand-in-hand, and opened the door to the lounge that had been decorated with birthday banners, streamers, and balloons, along with upbeat music playing on the stereo.

From then on, Sharron pretty much had the perfect birthday, and the Rose-Eccleby family day at the beach couldn't have come quick enough.

However, they had to get through the night first.

2

I am home, she thought. And stopped and trembled at the thought of how the house full of her childhood memories looked completely different...

Plink, plink, plink.

Whilst Isabella was in the midst of having the nightmare that made her tremble in her bed, Sharron Rose felt the dripping of the water once again. But this time, the entire ceiling made it rain. The bed was drenched and the house was not how it should've been.

The walls surrounding her closed in, all the carpets were torn away and replaced by creaky, wooden floorboards, and each door of the house swung back and forth barely on its hinges.

Anthony wasn't next to her in the bed. Sharron felt for the mattress underneath her, but there was nothing but the base there. She looked around the room, under the bed, and in the cupboards for a light of sorts as all the lights were off and not working. For a final time, she searched under her bed, feeling loose strands of fluff and muck instead of a torch. Sharron placed her other hand on the base of the bed to stay balanced on her knees, until...

You won't find what you're looking for.

Sharron smacked her head on the bed frame when she heard the voice of her mother. She stood up quickly and brushed the stains and muck off of her nightgown.

"What'd you want, now?" asked Sharron, going white as her nightgown.

Nothing that you don't know, responded Brenda, shrugging, and followed up with a slight cackle like a witch. Brenda sat cross-legged on the base of the bed, leaning upwards to her daughter. *You've been ignoring me. Why?* She pouted, overexaggerating her droopy lips and cat-like eyes. *You've hurt my feelings.* Sharron knew exactly what Brenda was trying to do: make her feel guilty for blocking out her mother's voice. *I just wanted to see you*, she whimpered fakely.

Sharron rolled her eyes and said nothing as Brenda stood up from the bed to look at her daughter dead in the eye.

"Now, what is it that you really want?" Sharron barked.

Like I said: nothing that you don't know, Brenda snarled.

The silhouette of Sharron's mother flew right through Sharron herself, the offspring feeling a gust of wind. Sharron turned as her mother's ghost stopped and turned back to her on the landing, gesturing for her to follow her down the rickety stairs and into the passage-way. As the ghost whooshed down, Sharron tip-toed her way across the landing and down the stairs, every creak louder than the last. The thought of waking Isabella did cross her mind but Isabella was in a *deep* sleep of her own.

Brenda patiently awaited her daughter at the bottom of the stairs, where she stood transfixed at the door that would lead them into the tip that was the lounge. They didn't enter straight away, though.

"What are we doing down here?" Sharron asked, curious.

You've left me no choice, but I now have to show you what happens when...

Sharron interrupted her, "When what?"

Well, you'll just have to see for yourself.

Sharron attentively watched as Brenda Rose's pale, ghost hand reached out for the doorknob and twisted it, clicking as the door creaked open wide. All Sharron could do was stand in the frame of the open door in scared amazement.

The lounge was a disgrace: moss grew on the walls as all kinds of insects scattered around the damp floorboards. Apart from the bucket loads of spiders, cockroaches, and dung beetles, there was only Sharron, Brenda, and the walls; the furniture that would have been neatly positioned had vanished, revealing cracked skirting boards and mouseholes. They both examined the room, Sharron with fear in her eyes and Brenda hiding a demonic grin as she looked up at the ceiling where the chandelier would have been shining stunning lights.

"Is this what you *only* wanted to show me?" inquired Sharron, looking at her mother who still stared at the ceiling with a cheerful smile on her ancient face. Brenda then turned to her daughter and, without saying a word, nodded in the direction of the centre of the ceiling to reveal a rope hanging from a hook, swinging back and forth.

Sharron gasped, gobsmacked and unable to say another word. Brenda cackled. What she saw dangling on the end of the rope was a lifeless carcass, possibly in their teens, the view of their face blocked by their flowing hair. The body swung back and forth with the neck snapped, in the grasp of the rope. And it was as if Sharron remembered, *Oh, right, I can scream.* And with Brenda suddenly gone, leaving Sharron alone in the lounge with the hanging body, she screamed. She screamed as loud as she could and tried to back away, but tripped over – what felt like – an invisible, small table, falling to the ground and...

CRASH.

The body was gone and the chandelier was back where it was. As a matter of fact, the sitting room – and the rest of Wardle Gardens – was back to its original, comfortable state. Sharron caught her breath as she tried to comprehend what she had just seen.

That person looks awfully familiar, she thought, just when she heard screaming and crying from upstairs. She heard frantic footsteps make their way across the landing.

"It felt so real," she heard her daughter cry out. Sharron focused on what was occurring upstairs and sprinted back up the carpeted stairs, storming into her daughter's bedroom, and noticing Isabella uncontrollably weeping and Anthony comforting her.

"Rose, where were you?" Anthony asked.

"I… I don't know," Sharron said, yawning away her daze and confusion as Anthony switched his attention back to their girl. During Anthony's explanation to Isabella that everyone has nightmares now and again, the vision of the disfigured body hanging from the rope came back to her. But this time, the person was more clear. It was as if the vision was happening right in front of her and the hair of the person swished to the side to reveal a sixteen-year-old Isabella Rose-Eccleby.

The vision vanished as quickly as it appeared.

"Really?" Isabella asked both of them, Sharron looked eager to reply.

"We all do, darling," agreed Sharron. "Ones about events that we don't want to happen." Her tone changed from soft and gentle to a tone that made her sound like she was in another trance. She looked like it, too, glaring above and around her daughter at the walls, panting as she felt them closing in.

I'll have to take one of you eventually, Sharron heard, making out that the voice was her mother, Brenda…

"You were saying you were going back to bed," lied Anthony, *stretching the truth* to his wife who had no clue what she had just said to Isabella, making her daughter feel even more uncomfortable than she already was.

"Oh, okay," Sharron said dismally, rising from her kneeling position next to Anthony and leaving without a fuss. Just about to cross the landing, Sharron glanced back at the partially closed door and said wistfully, "Are you sure you're okay?"

"Yes," Anthony barked rapidly, his raised voice echoing through the landing, assuring that Sharron didn't re-enter.

Sharron hung her head in shame as she barged through her own bedroom door and slumped onto her side of the bed, her face pushed deep into her pillow. And a few moments later, the door whipped open and Anthony entered looking half worried and half infuriated. The door slammed shut on its own accord from the might Anthony used to open it.

"What was that?" he said, demanding an answer, his arms folded. He did not take his eyes off of Sharron, his brows like two sharp arrows and his eyes were like slits of rage.

"I don't know," she answered, in between sniffs and deep breaths, her eyes starting to water frantically.

All Anthony could do was gently shake his head and sit down on his side of the bed, double checking that the bedroom door was closed.

"What-Is-Wrong?" he said clearly, clutching her hand and forcing her to sit up. "Whatever it is, we can sort it."

"I'm just not in the right state of mind at the moment," she squeaked, breaking down into a fresh pool of tears. *Stretching the truth* wasn't Sharron's favourite thing to do. "I think I need to clear my head, you know?"

"We've got the beach tomorrow, and then..."

"Then what?"

"Maybe you should take a little holiday, go with Dad, perhaps," he suggested timidly. Sharron looked at her husband and tried to hold back any further tears, and finally agreed with an unenthusiastic nod. "I think it's for the best." He rubbed her shoulder gently and they both laid down.

And after an hour of sleepless thoughts, both Anthony and Sharron dozed off wondering what the next day was going to deliver.

3

Running around in the cool, refreshing North Sea did make-up for the sweltering heat that this day had brought. It was a day when they had felt like a family.

Sharron and Isabella had been chased by the monster that was Anthony, who was threatening to gobble them up and cook them for his supper. They all laughed at Anthony's terrible impression of a monster as they splashed through the North Sea.

However, the moment of the Rose-Eccleby's being a family was gone as fast as it came. Isabella laughed breathlessly, rolling around in the water with her dad, oblivious to Sharron suddenly stopping and looking up at one of the far cliffs that stood at the ends of the beach. She was transfixed, yet still quite observant and aware of her whereabouts. But what she saw at the top of the cliff wasn't how Isabella remembered the day at the beach: Sharron gasped in fear, and saw the body of a sixteen-year-old Isabella floating at the edge of the cliff, dead, and – all of a sudden – the body fell in the piles of rocks and water that stood at the bottom of the cliff.

Sharron didn't scream or react. All she felt was nothingness, feeling as if she was gliding towards the horizon, oblivious of her body sinking as she walked deeper and deeper into the vast ocean, with a goal to reach where the sky meets the sea. She felt lifeless and wanted this horror to end. Sick of her life.

From one moment to the next, Sharron felt life wearing away until she suddenly felt a pair of hands dragging her back from the horizon. Sharron struggled to communicate, fighting her way through the hands – not knowing it was the hands of her husband.

"No!" Sharron bellowed, her voice at a pitch that Isabella had never heard before.

"Sharron stop!" Anthony ordered, dragging her to shore by the waist as Isabella just stood there, bewildered, and scarred.

"I've got to save her!"

That statement was completely ridiculous and out of context to Anthony and Isabella. Sharron had put up a fight, but Anthony was finally able to heave her back to land, saving her life from death.

"This is out of control," Anthony said, not wanting Isabella to hear. Sharron didn't respond, but nodded, crying. "Perhaps we should go to your father's for a few days?"

It sounded more like a demand rather than a suggestion, because all three of them were fully packed by dusk.

4: NOW

Sharron's silhouette had returned beside Isabella who stood at the gate of Wardle Gardens; they both saw it as night, watching the lost memory of the family driving away to Sharron's father's.

"I didn't know," Isabella said softly, watching her young self, dozing off in the backseat of the family car as they drove out of the drive. The ghost of her mother glanced at her daughter. "Only if you had told me."

You were six, defined Sharron. *As much as you think you could've helped, you couldn't have done anything*. Recollecting many lost and fond memories alike, they both stood in silence for a moment. Sharron, however, started to look anxious and glared at her daughter, as if she was split between telling her something or just brushing it past her. At the end of the day, the choice did involve the true reason why Sharron had come to Isabella at the bench and brought her to *their* home.

"Why did you really come to me, tonight, Mother?" It was like Isabella had read her mother's mind; well, in a dream you can do anything, can't you?

*Do you really want to know what happened 'that' nigh*t? Isabella turned to her mother, shocked, and they both suddenly went from outside Wardle Gardens to inside of the lounge. Sharron had to explain before Isabella could finally see what had been eluding her all these years. *I wasn't well*. They stood face-to-face by the doorway that led into the main passage. Isabella rolled her head around, noticing that the house was exactly how she remembered it. *My misery had to end*. They both started to cry as they turned their heads towards the floor where they saw Anthony kneeling over a prone body.

"Wh-What?" Isabella surprised herself with letting out a word, she was so shocked at what Sharron had shown her.

My misery had to end.

Sharron and Isabella continued to look down at Anthony, and the teen noticed that her dad was crying, cradling something in his hand. She tilted forward over Anthony's shoulder and saw that in his other hand he was holding the lifeless hand of her mother. She followed the arm up to the shoulder, up to the face, and there it was: a red dot in between her eyes, spreading across her face, her eyes wide open – but not awake.

"No. No. No. No. No. No." Isabella didn't want to believe it. It was only a dream, right? Or was it a lost memory?

5

Isabella Rose-Eccleby woke up drenched in sweat, her head sore from resting on the park bench and the drink from the party. It took a couple of moments to gather her whereabouts and realised that she was being watched by passing pedestrians with bouquets of flowers in their hands as they went to visit their passed loved ones. She breathed heavily as she wiped the sweat off her forehead, getting a glimpse of the beaming sunlight.

The sky was clear and the sun was almost directly above her. She wiped her face down and initially thought, *Dad's going to kill me*. As if nothing happened, Isabella left the graveyard and made her way back to her house, Chessington Close.

Or I'm going to end up killing him.

6

Her face was as red as burnt skin. Isabella had bottled up so much anger that it couldn't be contained.

Anthony hadn't greeted her with a "Hello." He went as far as to not even acknowledge her when she first crept in. Anthony had just sat there, motionless, at the head of the dining table. His hands were interlocked and his head was down. Isabella thought that she would be able to pass him without confrontation, but how wrong she was.

"Have fun last night?" said Anthony finally, standing up from the seat and marching towards his baggy-eyed daughter. Although she wanted to, Isabella couldn't say a word. She had no excuse, and all she could do was look directly down at her soggy shoes. "You know, I used to do that: creep out to go to parties." He walked around her like a police officer interrogating a criminal. "I ended up in a lot of trouble, but God how much I loved to do it." Anthony was talking clearly, but he wasn't shouting. In fact, he was quite patient with his daughter about the entire situation (mostly). "I bet it felt good, didn't it?" he continued. Isabella acted as if she was listening and replied with a loud cough, walking into the kitchen and taking a seat at the dining table. "I don't mind you going out with friends, but never in my life would I expect..."

Anthony froze, silence lay steadily in the room and spread across the whole of Chessington Close. His body fuelled up with anger that had passed its boiling point; he looked like he was going to explode, his face a bright purple. Isabella ruffled through her pockets and pulled out a filthy lighter, and that's when she finally locked eyes with her infuriated father.

"What?" she said unintelligently, shrugging her shoulders.

Anthony moved directly in front of his daughter, a fire lit in his eyes, and pointed dramatically at the next thing that Isabella had taken out of her pocket.

"What The Fuck Is That!?" he roared.

"A cigarette," she stated, placing it on the tip of her mouth and looked like she was just about to light it. "It's not lit," she added through Anthony's amplified breaths of pent up anger and disappointment.

"I know it's not lit, but why the hell do you have it?" Isabella could tell that Anthony was tempted to scream the house down, but tried his best to maintain his anger and just try and talk as calmly as any parent would in a situation like this.

"I bought it off a friend," she huffed in between puffs of smoke.

"Who? Hannah and Jess?"

"Ha! That's funny: buying a cigarette off Hannah and Jess. No, I got it off my *real* friends." With no ashtray in sight, Isabella carelessly stubbed the tip of the cigarette on the bare wood of the dining table. "They were holding me back; *you* were holding me back."

"What?!" Anthony exclaimed with a slight break in his voice. "What is wrong with you, Isabella?" Isabella shrugged and turned away. "Isabella, this isn't you." She turned back instantly, that look of anger growing inside her like the look Sharron would give him if he did or said something wrong. "If you're hiding something, you should just tell me," he assured in a more gentle tone than before, placing his hand on his daughter's shoulder.

She shrugged it off as quickly as she felt the tips of his fingers and stood up, alarming Anthony, and making him move back, intimidated.

"You want to talk about *hiding* things?" snarled Isabella. "Well, how about you, Dad. How about you tell me what you're hiding." Their noses were touching intensely.

"I don't know what you're talking about." Anthony said, once again stretching the truth. This time though was without a doubt the last straw.

"About Mother? What happened on *that* night? Doesn't ring a bell?"

As a matter of fact, it did ring a bell. Anthony denied admitting what he did on that night in Wardle Gardens. The memories came flooding back; the unforgettable memories of them all at the park, on holiday, and even sitting down in the evenings watching a film of Isabella's choice, all snuggled up together as a family.

That's when Anthony finally broke down into a heap of tears, brushing off Isabella to sit back down at the dining table with his face in his hands, overflowing them with constant tears. And through all this, Isabella didn't feel the slightest bit guilty.

"Oh, Isabella, this isn't you. I just wish you would go back to being the sweet, innocent girl you once were," he said after catching his breath and wiping away tears.

Isabella confidently walked up next to her seated father and made sure that this was truly hammering the final nail in the coffin.

"That girl is dead," she said deeply. And, without hesitation, her speech marked by close to no action, leaned even closer, her lips almost pressed against his ear, whispered, "And I wish that it was you that died and not Mother."

She strode off with conviction and grinned from ear to ear, her eyes like slits. That was until:

"GET OUT! GET OUT! GET OUT!"

Anthony had snapped. From tears to unbridled rage, Anthony chucked his chair, stood up and had started to hit anything in sight. Isabella had perhaps crossed the line herself from what she had witnessed before she made a run for it. She ran off and it was when she heard roars from inside the house that she started to feel the guilt set in. She thought that Anthony hadn't even noticed her leaving.

And after fifteen minutes of using the couch pillows as punching bags and stress relievers, he had started to calm down.

Three strikes and she's out. That was her third strike.

The voice echoed through Chessington Close, yet the source of the soothing voice could not be seen. Even Isabella had thought as she walked along to the end of the street that she heard a familiar voice, but couldn't make out what she said.

"I just wish she knew the full story."

Chapter Eight

Curtains Close

1: THEN

Scarred for life, Anthony had to walk back to Sharron's father's from Wardle Gardens as he too haphazardly crashed his car into the garage upon arrival as he followed Sharron.

His hands were covered in dry blood, like paint. He showed no emotion upon his return to the Rose household and he was surprised to see that Isabella was wide awake, sitting on a high stool in the kitchen.

The keys to the front door had been lost for a couple of days and the Rose family wasn't able to find a replacement, and so they said that the back door was officially the front door. Using the back door had been an advantage for anyone who had had a late night as the door was completely silent when it was opened. The first thing you would see when entering through the back door was the small utility room, where the washing machine and the dryer were kept, connected to the lengthy kitchen. Birch wooden cupboards stood against the wall and the bench tops were made of marble. Along the side wall opposite the only window in the room was the small, circular, black dining table with high stools to match.

However, the first thing that Anthony caught eyes with was her paranoid daughter. She sat there glaring at her father in the doorway, pondering what had happened on Anthony's outing. His scruffy clothes were potential giveaways.

"Just paint, sweetie," he lied, glancing down at the blood spread across his shirt and hands. Dry blood did oddly look like paint. Not wanting to spread it onto Isabella's nightgown, he led her outside when the sun had started to shoot its rays on Castlehead.

Trying to add a little light to the situation, he jokily bowed as Bella walked out and sat on the doorstep. Anthony closed the silent door behind them and sat with her for a few moments, panting and looking distressed.

"W-Where's Mother?" Isabella finally said, finding the courage to state the obvious.

"Asleep," he stuttered. "We're going to have to find a hotel for a few days, we can't stay here anymore."

All the time they spoke, they did not make eye contact.

"Where is Mother sleeping, Dad?" asked Isabella.

"*Home*, darling. *Home*," Anthony answered, aware of Isabella staring down at his painted hands.

Anthony sniffed and wiped his nose with the clean sleeve, hiding that he had drowned Sharron in a pool of his own tears after the incident.

"Can we go and see her?" Bella asked softly, looking at his marked face. It was as if he had been scratched by a cat. Anthony wanted to let her down lightly.

"No," Isabella made out by reading her father's lips. "We can't see her anymore," he said a little louder.

Isabella didn't need to ask what he meant by that, she was mature enough to know. She didn't cry nor ask how, all she did was sit there and take her father by the bloody hand and leant against his arm. His daughter's comfort felt nice and warm in the cool, morning breeze.

Ambient sound of sirens were heard in the midst of all the silence. Anthony knew what they were for (even though he wasn't the one that called them): to investigate Sharron's prone body and for it to eventually be taken to the mortuary, and to investigate the scream of death that came after the gunshot heard in Wardle Gardens.

"Why, Dad? Why?" whispered Isabella.

2

Two weeks later, it was an emotional day for everyone who personally knew Sharron Rose, especially for Anthony Eccleby and Isabella Rose-Eccleby. Like how most people felt once they heard the news that Sharron had died in a *serious accident*, it still didn't feel real to the six-year-old and her father.

The investigation of what actually happened the night Sharron Rose was found remained a mystery for ten years; no one had evidence that it involved Anthony, and no one suspected it either. People had said that it was an unfortunate event that can happen at the most unexpected of times and even to the happiest of people.

Yet, perhaps Anthony was expecting it. He knew that she wasn't well and wasn't herself, and some people can recover from hitting their breaking point but Sharron wasn't one of them; she knew she had to end it all.

Maybe he could've done more.

And shock spread across Castlehead after authorities had found the body in Wardle Gardens, reading the front page of *The Castlehead Chronicle*:

THE CASTLEHEAD CHRONICLE

DATE: 8/3/2009

The residents of Castlehead are saddened to hear the sudden news that the body of beloved citizen, Sharron Rose, was found dead early yesterday morning in the lounge of her home, Wardle Gardens, with a bullet wound to the head.

Authorities aren't certain why this unfortunate event has occurred so suddenly, but they initially suspect that it had been suicide.

We were unable to talk to her devoted husband, Anthony Eccleby, or her daughter, Isabella, but on behalf of Castlehead, we are sorry for your loss and we are all thinking of you at this sorrowful time.

Castlehead residents, family, and friends, are formally invited to attend Sharron Rose's funeral at Central Cemetery in two weeks' time, 22/3/2019, to pay their respects to one of Castlehead's most beloved citizens.

Isabella hadn't been allowed to read the article.

The funeral home wasn't large enough to fit all the guests during the service. Everyone who knew Sharron well had known about Sharron's popularity across the entirety of Castlehead, but even Anthony and Isabella were stunned to see what looked like half of the city waiting outside as they followed in a black limousine the hearse that carried her coffin.

During their slow, painful ride up to the cemetery, Anthony thought non-stop about that night and what Sharron had said to him before he ended it all for her, whereas Isabella didn't say a word until after the service itself.

Anthony and Isabella squeezed passed the tight queue to the front of the line waiting anxiously for the service to start. Anthony had requested for Harold, Sharron's dad, to walk in front of the coffin as the pallbearers carried the coffin into the single-level funeral home. Harold graciously accepted, but that was the last time they had talked.

The entrance song had begun, signalling the start of the service and Harold led the way into the funeral home – in a black suit, like all the other males, with the females wearing black dresses and fedora style hats – followed by the pallbearers and the closed casket.

Silence filled the room once everyone – the ones who managed to fit in – entered. Close relatives and friends sat in the front two rows of benches that stretched along most of the home, making Harold lead the pallbearers around the row of ten to the front and sit down with Isabella and Anthony in the centre of the front row.

The pallbearers placed the coffin down on a small, elevated stage, the length of the coffin, covered with purple fabric decorated with gold sequins, and stood either side of the home. Candles lit the room, hanging from torch brackets on the side walls. And when the director of the funeral home, Mr David Montague, stood on the podium, that was when the service had officially begun.

"Ladies and gentlemen, boys, girls, friends, and family, we are gathered together to remember the life of beloved daughter, mother, and wife, Mrs Sharron Rose."

By the time the service had ended, it was half past one in the afternoon; everyone bowed their heads in silence and slowly marched out of the funeral home to the exit song in columns of two. The candles dimmed and everyone burst into tears. And it was then when Anthony had gathered that Sharron's pain and suffering had ended once and for all.

If you really loved me, you would end my misery, Anthony recalled Sharron saying to him, whimpering aesthetically as he pointed the pistol that had been stolen from Harold's bedside cabinet at her head. He sealed her fate with one last kiss of death and then...

BANG!

And as the silent crowd exited the funeral home, Anthony felt a twinge in his neck. He felt the twinge turn into a sting and, making sure nobody noticed, squirmed around until he heard the conversant witch-like cackle of his mother-in-law.

I had to take her eventually. Did she really have to? Perhaps, to prove that she was willing to do anything to imply that she was right in one way or another.

"Why didn't you take me instead?" he said regretfully, through gritted teeth from the pain that shot down his neck.

You weren't mine to take.

3: NOW

Even now, two weeks after their heated argument, Anthony did not expect to be arranging a funeral for his daughter, Isabella Rose-Eccleby, just a short decade after they said goodbye to Bella's mother. Like the previous funeral, he felt like it didn't truly hit him until the service started.

Central Cemetery was where the funeral took place, two weeks after the argument and two weeks after Anthony saw her inanimate body swinging back and forth, eyes wide open, but not awake, as if she was staring into his soul.

It was awfully familiar, the position he was in on the tragic day resembled the first tragedy that struck the Rose-Eccleby family those years ago. He had taken his seat in the very front row and on both sides of him, he felt the comfort of the gentle touch of Jess and the sledgehammer hands of Hannah.

They all linked arms, his left arm tightly squeezed by the pressure of Hannah's grip. They cried together, they rejoiced as the funeral host recalled many of Isabella's most fondest memories, but most importantly, they were there for each other.

Walking out of the funeral home – arms still linked – to the chosen exit song, *Hold My Hand*, Anthony took the pair of Isabella's friends and the crowd of guests to where the burial would take place. Anthony requested for Isabella to be buried right beside Sharron Rose.

Everyone, in columns of two, took a slow walk up the pathway under the clear sky and blazing sun. The group of pallbearers did well to keep control of the coffin as they heaved it up to the newly dug grave.

The number of guests that came to pay their heart-warming respects wasn't even half of the number that appeared at Sharron's burial, however that didn't matter to Anthony. The ones who showed were the ones that mattered; even a small group of Isabella's teachers from her school turned up.

Standing around the freshly carved tombstone that read:

IN LOVING MEMORY

OF ISABELLA ROSE-ECCLEBY

and the seven-foot long, six-foot-deep, grave, the group made room for the pallbearers who arrived lastly.

As crows squawked and flowers blossomed, Anthony, Jess, and Hannah took their position at the front of the crowd to witness the coffin being lowered into the hole. The coffin was as red as a rose, ironically, and was smooth as a paving stone. Adjacent to the foot of the grave stood a pile of earth ready to be placed back into the grave at the end of the service. To make the scene more attractive for the guests, who stood honourably, the area surrounding the grave itself had been decorated with artificial turf. Placed delicately on the automatic lowering device, one staff member gave a signal to another who pulled a lever, activating the device and descending the coffin into the grave.

"Goodbye, Isabella," Anthony, Jess, and Hannah whispered synchronously, wiping away tears as they all watched Isabella – who lay dead in the coffin – cascading smoothly like a waterfall deeper and deeper into her final resting place.

No more pain, no more suffering – not for Isabella at least.

"Are you going to keep the letter?" Hannah finally said, walking beside Anthony as the three of them walked back down to the funeral home where all the cars were parked.

Awakened by the reality so much that he couldn't gather his surroundings, Anthony was heartbroken, therefore not replying to Hannah, or making himself visible to the crowd for the rest of the day and for the most part of his remaining life.

All Anthony had wished for was to tell her that he was sorry and wished that their relationship before Isabella's departure didn't end on such bad terms.

4: THEN

For the better part of a decade, no one knew the true horror that struck that night in Wardle Gardens; only Anthony was the secret keeper and didn't plan on revealing the traumatic event to anyone, saying when being interrogated that he knew that something was wrong but never thought that Sharron would go to drastic levels to kill herself.

"It was either suicide or a killing," the investigating officer said firmly. "So which one was it?" The officer marched around the fatigue Anthony, making him quiver. But that was something that he didn't want to show.

"Suicide," answered Anthony plainly.

The officer went on and on about that if a suicidal woman wanted to kill herself, she would point the gun at the side of the head, not go to the trouble of pointing the gun directly in between her eyes. Nonetheless, with every true suggestion made by the officer, Anthony denied these accusations and kept the truth sealed from the outside.

The officer wasn't convinced.

"Run the night by me one more time."

Anthony sighed and reluctantly retold the events that occurred the night Sharron Rose was killed.

5

It was the family's first night away from Wardle Gardens and at Sharron's parents. The sky was cast with clouds as black as coal that blocked the twinkling stars, and all Sharron did was sit in the front garden in a folding chair and gazed up at the night sky.

"Okay, are you sure?" Anthony overheard her say in a stammering voice. "Okay, I will." It was like she was agreeing to a deal or something.

The breeze began to pick up speed and whistled loudly. But once Anthony stepped into the cold, thin air, the gale stopped.

"Who are you talking to?" he asked curiously.

"What?" She turned in her chair suddenly. "Oh, no one, just myself," she said weakly, suddenly becoming aware of her husband's presence. She turned back around and stared at the row of identical houses across the road. "When we are born we are in death's grasp," she added shockingly.

Anthony helped her up without saying a word and carefully led her back into Harold's house, wanting her to get ready for bed.

It had appeared that the clouds had moved on, because the moonlight shone brightly through the window blinds. The television was on but nobody was actually watching it. Harold had dished up a basic dinner for the family before bed and went up without any food.

"Is he okay?" asked Anthony, turning to Sharron snuggling up on the couch next to a snoozing Isabella. Sharron didn't answer as she was dozing off herself, but all Anthony could do was smile at the sight of his two favourite people in the whole wide world.

He quietly put his empty plate on the kitchen worktop, switched the TV off, dimmed the light, and proceeded to a cupboard next to the fireplace in the sitting room, opened the wooden cabinet and pulled out a thin, cosy blanket that was admiral blue dotted with golden stars and a waxing crescent moon as yellow as a sunflower. Anthony laid the blanket on the mother and daughter, examined their beautiful faces, and went up to the spare room where he was sleeping.

The sound of Harold humming in the shower echoed through the upper floor of the house, and Anthony had changed into his nightclothes and whipped the duvet off his bed and lay down. He pulled the cotton duvet up to his neck and, his ears perked for the sound of anything suspicious, forced himself into a goodnight's sleep.

6

"And then what?" the detective asked, urging a worn-out Anthony to continue.

With bags under his eyes, Anthony gave out a howling yawn.

"And then about half an hour later – I want to say – I had been woken up by a loud racket coming from downstairs.

7

It felt like half an hour when it was really two quick hours. Anthony smacked his head on the headboard to the sound of a crash coming from downstairs.

Sharron, his immediate thought was, climbing out of bed and rushing down the staircase as quietly as possible, knowing that the stairs creaked louder and louder with every step. He burst through the door and saw that Sharron was no longer on the couch asleep next to Isabella. Isabella was out like a light; not even if a war occurred on the front step would she wake up.

"Sharron?" Anthony tiptoed past the couch that Isabella lay flat-out on and entered the kitchen to the sound of even more clangs and crashes. Barefooted, the stone floor was as cold as ice and had almost caused him to let out a high-pitched yelp like an opera singer. Luckily, he managed to contain it and noticed Sharron rummaging through a drawer under the kitchen sink. "Sharron?" he said, worried in the pitch black. What if it wasn't her?

"Oh, Anthony, hi." It was her, and the scavenging stopped. "What are you doing down here?" she asked alarmingly.

"The question is: what are you doing down here and making all this racket?" He walked towards his wife, whose hand was still scuffling through the drawer quietly.

"I... I... I was just... I was just looking..." She looked around the kitchen suspiciously, the moonlight that shone through the window above the sink being the only source of light. Her eyes glowed like emeralds.

"Looking for what?"

"Just for some paracetamol. Headache." She tried to give a persuasive smile that couldn't fool even the stupidest of people.

"Upstairs, I think," guessed Anthony.

"Oh, right. Upstairs. Great, thanks," she said quickly, pecking him on the cheek and making a run for their bedroom to search for what she was *really* looking for.

Anthony, wondering, walked to where Sharron had stood and glanced down at the drawer and his eyebrows suddenly rose. It was Harold's medication drawer and the first medicine on the top of the pile was a small bottle of closed paracetamol. He thought for a moment as he held up the bottle to the moonlight, looked back in the direction Sharron ran and back towards the bottle. He stood silent until a sudden thud echoed through the entire house.

It sounded like a door slamming shut.

Both Isabella and Anthony alike jumped out of their skins and ran straight for the living room window, peaked through the blinds, and witnessed the headlights of Harold's Smart car switch on and back out of the drive and zoomed off.

"What's going on? Where's Mother?"

They both backed away from the window and Anthony sat Isabella down onto the couch.

"Okay, this is really important," Anthony said firmly. "I want you to go upstairs and sit with Harold and tell him that Mother and Father are out on *business*. Understand?" He was serious and Isabella started to sniff. Anthony had no time left to waste and begged her for an answer. "Do you understand? Can you do that for me?"

"Dad, what's going...?"

"Shh!" her father interrupted. "Can you do that for me? And promise you won't leave this house."

All this time Anthony had his hands firmly grasped on Isabella's shoulders, shaking her for an immediate answer. Isabella finally, though unwillingly, nodded and was taken by the hand and shoved up the stairs by her father with a bit more force than he intended.

Isabella ran to the top of the stairs and Anthony was ready to leave to chase his wife down until Harold's voice, heard from the top of the stairs, stopped him in his tracks.

"What is going on?" he asked instantly.

"I don't know," his son-in-law quickly replied. "I heard a noise from downstairs and so I went to see what the commotion was, and it was Sharron. She said she was looking for tablets for her head."

"And then?"

"And I told her to look upstairs, because I'm sure there's some in the cabinet next to our bed."

"She wasn't looking for headache tablets, Anthony," Harold said knowingly. "She came into my room too. And whatever she had been looking for, she found it."

"And what was she looking for?" Anthony asked curiously.

"My gun," Harold replied regretfully.

And on that note, Anthony sped off out of the door leaving Harold and Isabella behind. He fiddled with the lock on his car door, impatiently trying to unlock it as fast as possible, started the engine, and drove off in the direction Sharron Rose had gone; he didn't need a map to know where she was going, too.

Anthony had headed straight for Wardle Gardens. The sky was clear and the moonlight made the house glow. It was like a checkpoint. But the sight that came with the house didn't make up the shining moon's light: Sharron had carelessly driven through the gates and, at full speed, crashed into the garage built at the bottom of the drive.

He parked his car askew on the pavement outside the house and ran as fast he could into the house. The front door had been left open and, from the passageway, Anthony heard weak cries like a puppy's.

The house was clean, but not homely. Without hesitation, he pushed the door open and entered the lounge where he saw Sharron stand, staring blankly out of the window as straight and upright as a plank, with gun in hand but lowered.

"Rose, think about what you're doing," said Anthony reassuringly, inching closer and closer to his wife, wanting to take the weapon off of her without causing any harm.

"I have, my love," she said, transfixed on the outside world. "For the first time ever, I'm thinking clearly." She snapped her head towards Anthony and gave a weak smile. She was smiling but she wasn't happy.

"Rose," he said more firmly. "You're not thinking clearly. This isn't the woman I married." Anthony gently grabbed Sharron's gun hand and slipped the gun away from her. Sharron moved back, Anthony moved forward, and they were face-to-face. "I want to help you, Rose."

"Help me? There is no way." Sharron started to laugh crazily which turned into an uncontrollable cry. "Actually, there is one way." Sharron, through watery eyes, was fixed on the handgun.

"No!" Anthony knew exactly what she meant and he wasn't willing to change the course of his family's life by doing the one thing that Sharron thought was the only logical solution to end the terror she faced.

"Please," Sharron wept, close to begging.

Anthony was split between going with his gut or his heart; his heart told him to chuck the gun away and at least try to work together to get through this, though his gut told him that if she wasn't going to die tonight, she would soon enough.

"I... I... I just..." he couldn't finish his sentence, lost for words and fearful of the outcome. He held the gun up and stroked it, getting a feel for the heavy, cold weapon that Sharron had brought. Sharron too stared at the gun.

"Anthony," she said warmly. "If you really loved me, you would do this for me." She directed Anthony's arm upwards to be level to her head, the gun pressing lightly in-between her eyes. Anthony lowered his arm, moved forward and sealed Sharron's fate with one last kiss.

He returned to his previous stance and aimed the gun at Sharron Rose's head. This was a shot that he wasn't going to miss, even with his eyes closed, the bullet was going to create a blood dot the size of a small pebble in between her eyes. Anthony turned his head, his arm trembling as Sharron exhaled her last breath; with this final breath, she released everything that had had her head spinning for the past couple of years. And with Sharron mouthing "I love you," just as Anthony's finger was on the trigger, she was ready to die.

It was the shot heard all around Castlehead and it wouldn't be for another ten long years that Isabella would finally learn the truth of her beloved mother, Sharron Rose.

8

"She had told me she loved me for one last time and then she forced me to watch her pull the trigger, and then she died."

Anthony was exhausted and unwillingly telling his story to the detective, desperately wanting to get back to Isabella and continue his life as a widow father, with the previous week buried, but still lodged, in the back of his head. And perhaps there was a slight hint at the thought of maybe it would have just been better to tell the truth.

As time moved on, Anthony tried to move on with it, but with all these *what if*'s racing around in his brain, he couldn't. Maybe it would have been better for Isabella's sake for her to know right away, not being told her father's secret and finding out at the worst possible time.

And from then on, as he made his way back to Harold's, he made a promise to himself that he would never tell a lie to his daughter again.

Chapter Nine

Strike III - And You're Out

1: NOW

"GET OUT! GET OUT! GET OUT!"

Isabella had never witnessed Anthony have an outburst of anger like when Isabella had told him that she wished that it was him that died, and not Mother.

She had made a run for it and escaped from the wrath of a monster going ballistic and throwing a punch at any stable object that he set his sights on. Isabella knew for a fact that this wasn't the monster that had chased her and Sharron around at the beach those many years ago.

Having nowhere else to go, she had the intelligence to lay low and walk around the areas of Castlehead where she wouldn't dream of ever going. Isabella knew by doing this that Anthony wouldn't be able to find her.

2

The vulnerable girl was alone, weak, and tired as dusk settled. Some may even say she was isolated. As the evening drew closer, the sky turned a translucent orange, but, soon enough, the sky had been covered by devilish clouds as black as coal and clashed, causing the world to shake as thunder rang through her ears. A storm was brewing and it would be about time that Isabella had to find some shelter.

Nobody was out as rain started to pelt down, but it was like nails had been hitting the top of Bella's head.

Anthony had calmed down by the time the storm had fully taken a toll on the Castlehead conditions, and he was getting worried. That was when he courageously ran from the door to the car with no hood and went on the search for his daughter.

The only solution for Isabella was to go back to Chessington Close and hope that the atmosphere had calmed down since earlier that day. She was soaked and the storm clouds had made the evening sky look like midnight. Anthony wasn't home and Isabella managed to enter the house by the spare key that Anthony had always hid in the nearest plant pot just in case he was ever out and she was home before him.

Glasses had been smashed and chairs had been flipped, and Isabella thought it was the right thing to do to clear up the mess that was caused by her father's temper. Water had dripped from all corners of her clothing and her soggy hair, but she hadn't changed into fresh ones as she knew she wouldn't be staying long.

Thoughts of Sharron and what they were like as a normal family sprung to mind when Isabella sat on the foot of her bed, pen, and paper in hand. She had an idea of what she was going to write, yet couldn't produce the words and put pen to paper.

In the end, Isabella knew she had to get her feelings heard before she did something drastic, and making sure the coast was clear of Anthony, she wrote:

I really didn't want it to come down to this but I felt like this was something I had to do. For the past ten years I have tried constantly to live like the happy girl everyone knew me to be, but for the past ten years, I have felt like I have been living hell on Earth. I have felt like something has been missing from my life and that something is my mother.

There is a point in everyone's life when they hit their breaking point, and some can handle it better than others. Some, on the other hand, like me, feel like it's best to just end it once and for all.

Once you read this, I will be at MY home of Wardle Gardens. And if you do wish to find my body, I wish to be buried next to Mother.

Nobody truly knows what people are going through because everyone is afraid to speak up. Be nice to everyone and, most importantly, don't feel alone. There is no harm in sitting with someone and asking how they are or how their day is going, because you never know, it just might make their day. It might just change their life.

Finally, I would like to say thank you for the unforgettable memories, and I can't apologise enough for the strain and effect this will have on you all. But believe me, in the long run, you'll realise that it's for the best.

I love you Jess. I love you, Hannah. And most importantly, I love you, Dad.

Thank You, Isabella Rose-Eccleby. Xx.

3

Isabella had left the letter on the dining table for Anthony to read once he had finally returned from his search.

He pulled up in the drive and noticed that the lights in the house were on. Anthony investigated and hoped that Isabella was home. He entered to complete silence, calling out her name and pleaded for a response.

Anthony had searched all over the house, but Isabella wasn't there. He paced steadily back and forth in and out of the kitchen, formulating a plan, not noticing the newly written letter for him that rested on the table. Finally spotting it he picked it up and read it intently.

The letter fell out of Anthony's hand unintentionally and he had to maintain his balance as he had nearly collapsed in shock. His next move was undetermined, processing what he had just read. The letter lay on the floor in front of him and Anthony had hoped to God that this was some cruel prank Isabella had played.

But it was no joke; Isabella had made up her decision and it felt like there was nothing else she could have done to make her situation any better. And although forcefully anticipating the image he would have to confront when entering Wardle Gardens that night, he was completely oblivious to what he had to face in the future: the stages of grief.

Chapter Ten

The Fifth Stage of Grief

1

I am home, she thought. And this time, she stopped and felt relieved at the thought; the thought of how her home, Wardle Gardens, looked exactly the same from the outside. Isabella Rose-Eccleby didn't stop and hesitate to enter like she did in her recurring nightmares, she bravely stepped forward and faced the ghosts of her past. She had learned what had happened on that fateful night when her mother, Sharron Rose, had been killed, and now it was time for her to accept her own fate.

It was only when she had finished the letter that Isabella had convinced herself to thoroughly admit – to herself, not her father – that Chessington Close, yes, was a house that she lived in, but was not a home. Wardle Gardens had been her home and something had always been telling her that.

Isabella didn't need to knock. The moon was shining high, with the storm eventually passing, and she imagined lights from within drawing her to come closer and enter the house. And so, she did exactly that.

The reality was that Isabella was not leaving her home, Wardle Gardens, with her soul intact.

2

Anthony had found Isabella, at home, mangled and hanging from a rope that she had tied to the chandelier in the lounge. After cleaning up the vomit he had spewed up at first glance, he had untied her and carried her limp and lifeless body into the back of the car and took her to the hospital. He didn't need a doctor to tell him that she had killed herself, but it was them who had to give the body to the funeral home.

And like Isabella had wished in the letter, she had been embalmed and buried next to Sharron Rose in Central Cemetery.

3

Weeks had passed since the burial of Isabella Rose-Eccleby and there had been talk around the town that Anthony hadn't come to terms with reality yet, denying the fact that Bella had ever killed herself and telling himself that she – along with Sharron – would come back to him in time.

Then, it had been a month and Anthony had appeared to stop with the nonsense about Isabella and Sharron coming back to him. However, he had become angry. Very angry; angry at Sharron for being mentally unstable, angry at Isabella for thinking that she couldn't talk to him, and angry at himself for finally coming to the conclusion that he could have done more but had let everything slide and pan out, all because – deep down – he had felt nothing was sincerely wrong with his wife and daughter.

Several months of Anthony acting up like this had transpired, and his neighbours on Chess Street had started to wonder if he was starting to feel better, seeing him more often. Perhaps this was the turning point for him, perhaps he could be accepting the fact that this is just what happens in life. The only days he had gone back to feeling sorry for himself was on special occasions such as birthdays and Christmas; countless questions had come to mind along with the scenario of whether or not it would have been better if he had never been involved.

It was as if he was living in a nightmare.

Maybe Sharron's mother was right all along.

Life had completely changed for him, he wasn't bringing in an income and there had been reports that people wouldn't see him over a long period of weeks. Only on those rare occasions when he had to would he leave his house. Even speculation had arisen; a rumour had quickly spread that Anthony had killed himself, too. But this person had obviously created the rumour for his own wellbeing, doing it as a joke to impress his two cronies. This rumour had even gone as far as making itself on the news.

It was on a quiet day – during one of Anthony's isolation periods – that this rumour had famously made itself on the news. Anthony had joked to himself that he felt like death so he was half way there. But it was later on in the report, when a picture had cropped up of the Rose-Eccleby family, when Anthony fell back and had an epiphany: *This isn't what Sharron and Isabella would want me to be doing with my life.*

He rose from his seat, away from the discarded crisp packets and empty beer bottles, and pressed his face up against the television when the picture was up. The picture was of him, Sharron, and a baby Isabella. He fondly remembered the day that photo had been taken: it was Isabella's first time at the park and Anthony had videoed his wife and daughter racing down the slide, Isabella on Sharron's knee laughing away like the innocent girl everyone knew her to be.

"Now, if these rumours are true," the reporter said, reading from a script, and continued, "that would mean that this so-called *curse* has impacted him, too, proving that none of the Rose-Eccleby family could accept the reality that is life."

Acceptance? He thought. *I am willing to accept it, because now I know that I can keep them alive through memories*. That's when he had figured it out:

Acceptance is recognising the reality that our dear loved ones are physically gone. It is the new norm, which we must eventually learn to live with. People cope with death in different ways, and that's okay, but it all leads to acceptance. Nobody should be afraid to speak up about how they're feeling about anything that is on their mind; in the moment, some feel that they can't, and that is also okay, because they don't want to hurt the ones closest to them.

But if we communicate and come together, the ones who are suffering may not find the realisation any easier, but the learning curve will surely take a toll.

Our loved ones that we have lost may be gone physically, and, without their presence, it can change an atmosphere. But the memories and stories that we pass down is what keeps them and their spirit alive in our hearts.

THE END.

Lightning Source UK Ltd.
Milton Keynes UK
UKHW012351230920
370411UK00002B/35